WINTER'S LAMENT

BY:

Joyce A Brown

Dedicated to:

Cheryl Marie (Chip) Box

I miss you and our conversations.

What's really going on over at The Cathedral?

Charismatic Pastor Reese Thompkins transformed a struggling congregation in Central Illinois into a megachurch. When Pastor's not preaching and teaching, he's singing and producing music with an internationally recognized Gospel Choir that's been nominated for a Stellar Award. And by his side is his beautiful wife, Sister Kamilah, renowned children's author and artist. To the Christian Community, the power couple are sterling examples of marital harmony, and evangelists that can change lives through the mighty Word of God.

Behavioral Psychologist Dr. Annorah Sherman, can't believe anyone is naïve enough to buy this fairy tale. How did Pastor Reese show up, straight out of Bermuda, and create this liberal-leaning oasis? What secrets lurk behind the doors of The Cathedral? The International Truth Institute has bankrolled her investigation of Pastor Reese. Her revelations will propel her to the top of a media empire.

The hottest places in hell are reserved for those who in times of great moral crises, maintained their neutrality.
Dante 1265—1321

The secret things belong to the Lord our God; the things revealed belong to us and our children forever, that we may follow all the words of the law. Deuteronomy 29:29

CHAPTER ONE
REESE

REESE THOMPKINS' WATCH BEEPED for the third time in fifteen minutes. Being late for his meeting with The Cathedral's deacons was not the method he'd planned to gain their approval of a five-million-dollar project to rebuild the broadcast tower damaged eight weeks ago in November 2014 when a tornado ravaged Washington, Illinois. As pastor maneuvered down the long hallway leading to the boardroom, he accepted the holy handshakes, hugs, and kisses from the mothers of the church and high fives from the congregation's young people. Stuffed in the pockets of his robe were the checks and cash the women pressed into his hands. He'd sort the money later and donate it to the youth ministry. He directed the young people to assist the women to their cars and to remove the rapidly falling snow from their car windows.

Finally alone, Reese dropped his head for a moment of prayer, knowing chaos and sharp critique awaited him on the other side of the cherry wood doors. Seven years ago, the floundering church welcomed Reese into the ministry as an associate minister. He'd purchased a portion of the rural church's property to create a music studio and production company for his traveling music group. Three years ago, the founding pastor, Rev. Dexter Winston, died of sudden cardiac arrest. Reese was appointed senior pastor in a split decision. Although he was an anointed preacher, the deacon board questioned and debated every proposal brought to them by the ambitious pastor. His supporters were quiet men who approved of the changes to put the church on solid financial footing, voting as he requested, but unwilling to spar with the nay-sayers: founding church members Grimm and Hudson who, prior to Reese, held the reins of power in the church. Head Deacon Slay attempted to rule like Solomon, which was a challenging feat amid one-dimensional thinkers.

Reese opened the conference room door and quickly read the body language of the eleven men assembled around the oval mahogany table. The deacons either lounged in comfortable chairs or held themselves stiffly upright in front of the remains of healthy mini sandwich wraps and glasses of orange, cranberry, or pomegranate juice.

"Gentlemen, I apologize for my tardiness. Members of the congregation wanted to wish me well in the new year."

"Pastor, this meeting is unnecessary. The city and county don't control our purses over here. I say we repair the Tower and let it go," Deacon Grimm groused, squinting against the blinding sunlight reflected off the snow through the glass. Deacon Marcelle Grimm intimidated people with his bulk, his education, and his ability to make the kind of financial contributions most people of faith desired to give. "Look at where we are—new members, renovations, all these new programs."

Before Pastor Reese instituted a mandatory review of income and compulsory tithing, the deacon was a rainmaker in the church. He never let anyone forget it. In addition to his high paying job as director of finance at Peoria County, Grimm had been an early investor in several real estate developments. Based on insider information, Grimm sold his interests before the market softened because of manufacturing job layoffs.

"Did you read the inspection reports?" Reese pointed to the proposals spread out on the table. Reese's lips curved into a smile to take the sting out of his words. He ran his hand through his short black hair, the hint of natural curl reminding him he needed a haircut. "Deacon Grimm, a patch job will last less than a year. That's wasting money. It's in our best interest to take advantage of the newer technology standards."

State-of-the-art broadcasting infrastructure was instrumental to The Cathedral's ability to increase financial support from around the world. Undeterred by the men's less than welcoming gazes, Pastor Reese walked the church leaders through the severe damage caused by the hundred-mile-an-hour winds that toppled trees. Those falling trees knocked out wires connecting The Cathedral to broadcast and cable television as well as audio, public safety, land and mobile radios, emergency backup generators, and the Internet. After outlining his plan to raise the money, Reese spread his hands and said, "If an old reprobate like Johnny Swagger can use his television network to raise four-point-five million dollars in four days," he paused dramatically, "surely The Cathedral can use its network, friends, and corporate partners to raise five million dollars in thirty days."

"You are asking for too much money. It's more than we've ever done, and you're doing it right in the public eye. We're too vulnerable to failure." At eighty years old, Deacon Lee Roy Hudson refused to accept the status of Deacon Emeritus. The retired chemist's thin hair had been dyed so many times the gray roots showed through brown and red hair. After speaking his piece, Deacon Hudson pushed back his chair and walked over to the credenza where the picked over trays of food sat. He picked up two each of the chicken and ham sandwiches, grabbed a bottle of water, sat back down, and ate his second meal.

Reese arched an eyebrow at Hudson who was wearing the same shiny black suit he wore most Sundays. Hudson and Grimm could be counted on to eat more than their share of the food and speak on all issues, whether they were complaining or spouting ignorance. He conceded raising five million dollars in a month's time was a stretch even for him. However, this was a new year, and Reese's position was nonnegotiable. This was his farewell project, even if the deacons didn't know it. Reese was moving on with his life plan.

The young preacher pressed his agenda. "We burned the mortgage on this building." While still an associate minister, the church capitalized on Reese's musical genius to create mind-boggling music and produce concerts. Reese was a master at organizing inspiring music shows to bring in revenue and enticing unsaved people into the house of God. His shows brought together people across a broad socioeconomic and racial spectrum for a spiritual and emotional roller coaster ride.

"We're getting attention from people who've never set foot on the campus. One benefactor donated two thousand acres of adjacent farmland that's been in his family for years. It will expand The Cathedral's territory," Reese reminded the men with varying degrees of faith, experience, and education. They were not easily led. They were better suited to bullying pastors. "No strings attached."

"That land doesn't answer the question of how we gonna raise five million dollars." Deacon Albert Broadnax was an accountant at Illinois Central College. His features were beautiful when taken one at a time but too small for his block head. He was young, brash, and cheap except when it came to clothing and his car. "These folks are still reeling from the tornado."

Reese swallowed, fighting to control his temper while keeping his face straight. The rebuilding project was his last fight with this group. "We will use some of the money raised to support the people hardest hit by the storm. Insurance and government assistance got the homeowners back in their homes but did little to replace furniture and clothing they lost." He paused, counted to ten to control the tick in his cheek. "The renters and squatters are barely making it on what the Red Cross and other agencies have contributed. Two hundred displaced families who were living on the margins before the twister are still sheltered in The Cathedral's campus housing and eating in our cafeteria. They depend on us to feed them physically and spiritually."

The Cathedral's and Pastor Reese's benevolence was not an issue here. During this harsh economic climate, the church was living out one of its missions through the provision of direct services to the community, regardless of the church affiliation of those requesting the assistance. Knowing not to go down that street again, the cheapskate deacon asked, "How we gonna raise this money?" Broadnax's whiny voice grated on the other deacons' nerves.

Reese pointed to the folders in front of each man. The pastor had picked through lists of previous donors, advertisers, other ministries. The Cathedral's talented staff could develop fundraising materials and contact potential donors. He ran the numbers and this amount was doable. "We're going to make this happen with seed donations from the congregation and then launch a worldwide campaign for the balance. We'll be depending on social media; we will target individuals and corporations by relying on the name recognition we've garnered from music sales. We can raise five million dollars."

"There's a limit to what you can accomplish, Pastor Reese." Grimm's piercing eyes were cold. His clenched jaw could've been used to crack the leftover shelled pecans in the Hawaiian Kao wood bowl on the conference table.

"There are no limits on what God can do." Reese was a living testament to God's power. "What's the objection, gentlemen?"

Deacon Willie Ray Jones worked on the shop floor at Caterpillar. He turned away from the scowl Reese made no effort to conceal. "Brother Pastor, we ain't opposed to your suggestion."

Many heads nodded. Jones continued. "You are young. You don't understand people. Wait a while before springing this on the people." Jones glowered out the window at the snowdrifts. "It's January. People are repaying for overspending at Christmas and bracing for the high heating bills they are getting from CILCO. Energy bills ain't no joke."

"Gentlemen, did you listen to the presentation?" Reese pushed his chair back, stood and walked to the credenza to poured himself a cup of fragrant black coffee. He took a sip to allow himself a mini timeout. "Do you question God's timing?"

"No," Richardson responded.

"Harrumph." Hudson scowled.

Gesturing with his cup, Reese snapped, "He gave me the vision. He will deliver the provision." He took in the measure of each man. His deceased father used to say he didn't believe in scratching where he didn't itch. "I'm the shepherd of this house."

"We ain't never done nothing this ambitious before." Jones didn't make spur-of-the-moment decisions.

"Gentlemen, do you expect me to ask your permission to do God's work?" Reese drank his coffee, inhaling the aroma while reining in his anger and aggravation.

"We can't go along with this," Jones shouted. The other deacons nodded along with him.

Head Deacon Henry Slay, the even-handed moderator, called a halt to the bickering. "Deacons, read the proposal. We can discuss the merits. Nothing's going to be decided today." Slay retired from Caterpillar, the community's largest employer, and maintained a small insurance company to keep active. Slay assessed each man, his gaze lingering on Grimm. "The wife has supper waiting for me, and with the weather gettin' worse, we all need to get home." Recently, his kidneys failed. He was taking dialysis three days a week while praying for a donor. "First Lady will have our heads if we keep whipping on the pastor. Y'all know he don't eat until after the services." Slay placed a fatherly hand on Reese's tense shoulder. "Brethren, let God lead Pastor Reese. Our job is to support the pastor."

The room temperature was frostier than the blizzard outside as the deacons closed their folders and pushed them to the center of the table. Brother Slay stood up, put on his winter coat and hat. Deacon Slay's departure from the table signaled the end of the meeting.

"Good afternoon, gentlemen."

CHAPTER TWO:
NOORI

"Your proposal for an exposé on the harm these religious perverts cause was a stroke of genius, Noori." Dr. Thaddeus Sherman spoke from the head of the antique cherry dining room table.

Behavioral psychologist, Annorah Sherman, *Noori* to her family and friends, yearned to be anywhere other than the stately old Lakeshore Street mansion along the shores of Lake Michigan near the campus of Northwestern University in Evanston, Illinois. She didn't appreciate the magnificent mature trees bracketing the grounds. More than the cold outdoors, freezing ice, and snow-packed streets, she dreaded the ritual of Sunday dinner with her parents. Noori and her pseudo socialite mother, Portia, would've been more comfortable eating in the family's beautiful kitchen. However, Thaddeus Sherman's ideas resembled those of the fifties-era television show *Father Knows Best*. He grilled her about the executive research position he'd secured for her, her inability to find husband number two, and the details of her social life.

Sherman could have passed for white if not for his Negroid nose. His egg-shaped head was bald, and he sported a gray beard. He'd graduated first in his Morehouse class and earned a Ph.D. in Chemistry from Yale. He was a chemist for one of the largest manufacturers of HIV/AIDS drugs. Pharmaceutical drugs were paying off big in the markets. He secured several pharmaceutical patents in his name, and a prestigious position at one of the major pharmaceutical labs in the region. Daddy-dumbest, as she and her brothers referred to him because of his outdated ideas about black people and

8

the world in general, used his insider connections to make millions in the stock market.

When Noori's two older brothers and their families were in residence, the brothers deflected the patriarch's attention away from her. Today, the sons declared they were spending the day with their in-laws, probably watching football, and drinking imported beer. She, on the other hand, had to listen to a rehash of today's sermon. Daddy was about making money and propelling his agenda forward against black preachers who disagreed with his reactionary end time's fire and brimstone theology.

Today, she'd been drawn into a repetitive discussion about the International Truth Institute where her father was a founding board member and benefactor. The Institute's research staff was comprised of religious fanatics, failed theologians, and communications experts looking for exposure in a polarized country grappling with issues of religion, sexuality, and science. Noori wrote a weekly blog consisting of her research as well as that of right-leaning organizations, church gossip, social media scandals, and police news blogs dedicated to outing pastors for sexual misconduct.

Noori pushed her tinted glasses up slightly and pinched the bridge of her broad nose. "Whoop de doo." She was nursing the after effects from too much New Year's partying. Noori wasn't up for a discussion about her role in collecting the data necessary to undermine the work of men who disagreed with her father's views on homosexuality, on women in the ministry, and the demonization of unwed mothers. Daddy-dumbest had spent years grooming her and her brothers, egg-headed pale imitations of him, to think and act like some throwbacks to W.E.B. DuBois' racial notions of the talented tenth.

"Would you prefer the salmon or something else, Miss?" Pushing a serving cart, the Latina cook asked quietly. From previous days off with no pay, she knew not to serve foods Noori didn't eat.

9

"I'll have the lobster bisque and a salad." Noori hated these stuffy Sunday dinners. What she wanted was a dark bedroom and an ice pack. If she wasn't careful, her demons were going to drag her into Lake Michigan.

The brown-skinned woman served the daughter first and moved on to serve plated dishes of salmon, mixed vegetables, and quinoa to her parents.

"Let's pray." Dinner began with her father blessing the food and ended with rebuking the pastor of their church for his liberal leanings. Her father shot a 'what the hell' look as Noori picked up her soup spoon.

If the pastor's so ill-informed and ignorant of the true meaning of God's words, why not leave the church and go somewhere else. No, Thaddeus wasn't leaving because the church had an exclusive status where men like Dr. Sherman were touted as black community leaders based solely on education and income. His tiresome voice interrupted the drumbeat of her headache.

She'd zoned out when he started praying. Her father's smile did not reach his eyes. She snapped back in time to hear his announcement. "We spent New Year's Eve with some of Harrison's college buddies."

Harrison Lord was her father's business partner and chief fundraiser. Staunchly fundamentalist and reactionary Bible-thumping Christians, Lord family money and connections funded two-thirds of The Institute's Religious Liberty research agenda. The man was on a first name basis with every conservative legislator in Washington, DC. "Harrison wrangled another two-million-dollar commitment for your project to bring to light religious leaders who prey on unsuspecting people, cheat congregations out of their money, have multiple sex partners, and blaspheme the Word of God."

Noori knew what was expected of her. "Please thank Mr. Lord for his ongoing support. I will send him a note tomorrow as well as an updated brief on my progress to date."

The elder Sherman beamed. "The production team has set up a series of meetings. They want to see how you relate to live and videotaped audiences."

Noori was photogenic. Five feet six, medium brown skin tones, and feminine with shapely legs and broad hips. She worked out regularly. "Did you tell them I can walk and talk at the same time?" Noori needed street-level drugs and two scotches to endure this madness. "I do have a Ph.D. in Behavioral Psychology."

Why is your daddy paying your bills if you all of that?

"What you have is a hangover." Thaddeus' hand shook. He glowered at her. "Your sponsor says you've stopped going to your AA meetings. Take off those damn sunglasses in this house."

She complied. "Why is the organization's name Alcoholics Anonymous if your buddy reports back to you whenever I miss a meeting?"

Her mother gasped as she saw Noori's bruised eye which was now black, blue, purple, and a tinge of yellow. Earlier this morning, when Noori stared into her make-up mirror, the socket appeared ready to snap into sharp pieces.

Portia put down the forkful of salmon and spoke to her youngest child as if she were the pet terrier. "A. Black. Eye. Juvenile at best."

Her mother's position was Thaddeus is the breadwinner, and his money allowed her to live luxuriously without working outside the home. Her mother pursed her lips and turned up her nose. "Annorah, all we ask is you behave like the daughter we raised you to be." She dismissed her daughter without any inquiry about what happened. No sympathy. "You are an alcoholic, Annorah." Portia rolled her eyes at her daughter and lashed out. "With the money investments your father has secured, you will do whatever the investors require." Portia picked up her fork and resumed eating as if the matter were settled.

"Humph." Noori ate. The fragrant creamy soup soothed her nervous stomach and gave her a reason to remain quiet.

"The investors insist on photo testing, voice, and diction training. They might change your hair and make-up to increase your brand, your platform, and make you more appealing to test audiences."

Her brand was digging in the garbage of other people's sexual lives, financial maneuvering, drug use, and depravity. The brand took a toll on her own shaky hold on reality. "You and these geezers have lost your rabid minds." Noori rubbed her shaky hands across her forehead, closed her eyes, and waited for the pain to subside. She huffed, "I did the research, writing, and behind the scenes sleuthing to set up these stings."

Wait a minute, girlie. This new development of eminent funding might be beneficial after all. Maybe it was time to jab at the principal subject and remind the preacher it wouldn't be long before the kill shot hit between his beautiful eyes.

Her father continued to badger her. "The shock value and the audience reaction hinges on you coming across as a morally upright professional who's concerned about the religious values taught to our young people and the inappropriate behavior of their religious leaders."

"Morally upright...?" Noori's laugh was tinged with acid and hysteria. "Where does divorced and alcoholic fit in with morally upright?"

"This syndicate is bankrolling your cable television show to counteract the liberal agenda. You have the face and the credentials from two prestigious universities. If needed, they'll put out a story about the unsuitability of marrying the wrong man causing you to seek assistance."

"Didn't you tell them Dolton was your handpicked husband candidate?" Noori tossed that tidbit in his face like a bottle of lye—meant to burn and kill. She pointed her soup spoon at both parents. "Aren't you two still friends with his family?"

"Girl, I'll slap the taste out of your mouth." An enraged Thaddeus stood up and strode toward her seat.

Why did she provoke him? They'd been doing this same song and dance for too many years now. Noori implored her mother, "You gonna let your husband talk to me like—"

Portia's bored voice interrupted her. "Daughter, if he'd a listened to me when you divorced Dolton, you wouldn't be living in Hyde Park on our dime. There's always space for one more drunk at the women's shelter in downtown Evanston."

Her father stood behind her chair, hands gripping the chair's velvet back. Anger rolled off him in waves. "Civilized black folks are not accepting same-sex marriage or gays in the church parading around in leadership roles." His massive right hand moved forward and gripped her shoulder, "You are going to be the spokesperson for a whole new generation…which means you will do whatever the producers tell you to do."

Including spreading lies and propaganda.

"We want the perverts locked up in jail. We want to discredit churches protecting pedophiles, cross-dressers, and all sorts of closeted sickos ramming their godless ideas down our throats. We intend to convince the appropriate people of the need to return to the original listing of homosexuality as abnormal behavior."

CHAPTER THREE:
KAMILAH

INSTEAD OF WAITING TO serve Sunday dinner consisting of Bermuda shark prepared with mustard greens, peppers and onions, Kamilah and Reese were supposed to be in Palo Alto California, settling into her new apartment before Sofia University's Interpersonal Psychology program term started at the end of January. When she came to The Cathedral, Reese promised it would be for two years. Rather than sit idle while Reese schmoozed, charmed, and prayed his way through his agenda, she put her first-rate education from Bermuda College and Savannah College of Art and Design to good use.

Kamilah's threw herself into developing educational programs for many of the hurting children who came to the church. The secure campus was a hub where parents entrusted their physical and moral safety to the youth leaders. The Cathedral's youth ministry provided life skills classes, purity classes, mixed-martial arts, sports, leadership development, and service-learning opportunities.

The youngsters loved her watercolor sketches depicting three friends: a girl and two boys growing up in Bermuda. The faces were blurred, but the emotions they evoked were real. The sun-washed gold and blue canvasses illustrated scenes of the three children, swimming in the Atlantic Ocean, building sandcastles and flying kites. Pictures of the two boys playing dueling pianos while the tween girl twirled around them in a tutu. The joyful bond between the three was unmistakable. The last two pictures were different. The smaller boy and the girl, arms interlocked, stood on the shore watching a cruise ship disappear over the horizon. The final image was of a teen girl and a teen boy entwined in each other's arms, standing on a boat pointed to the mainland. Who and where was the missing boy in each of the last two pictures?

This past October, Kamilah, complete with photographs of her paintings and books, had been featured in three Christian literary magazines. Book sales quadrupled; she'd been invited to speak at six upcoming national youth meetings. She'd also been offered a weekly televised show on one of the Christian stations. She politely declined all the offers.

When Reese finally entered their suite of rooms, Kamilah searched his deep chocolate, clean-shaven angular shaped face, his thick eyebrows, and gleaming white smile for signs of battle. At five-foot-ten, Reese was whipcord thin with a swimmer's upper body strength and long, runner's legs. He was dressed in a custom-tailored black suit and handmade shoes imported from Europe. "Reese, the deacons aren't with you on this project?"

"The *no* came through loud and wrong." He changed out of his suit into navy pleated slacks and a blue button-down shirt. He never knew when he'd be called out to assist a member or someone would call and ask for an impromptu meeting. More importantly, his tailored wardrobe and fastidious appearance were as much a part of him as the faith in God he demonstrated every day.

Sunday was the one day she didn't work in her studio. As soon as Reese sat down and blessed the food, she passed him the shark dish. He inhaled soy sauce, garlic, balsamic vinegar, and parsley as he added greens to his plate. "These smells remind me of home."

Kamilah's food choices were deliberate: remind him of happier times in Bermuda. Rather than her everyday china, Kamilah used The Winston House's beautiful china, stemware, and heavy silverware on the weekends and special occasions. The ambiance wasn't working today.

Reese decoded the hostile body language, hidden agendas, and outright lies going on in the magnificently appointed boardroom until Kamilah wanted to hit him with the blood orange Cruset pots containing their dinner. "Reese, why are you fighting this battle? You can't lead goats any more than you can herd cats."

Kamilah stared intently at the man she'd loved forever, searching for the words to reach him. She had to make choices that put her first. Unable to deny him anything, Kamilah had allowed him to manipulate and twist her love. She was thirty-four years old without a home of her own.

"Let it go, Reese. No one expects you to be a martyr for this madness." She leaned a little closer, forcing him to see the newfound determination in her eyes.

"It's just a few more months, Milah. Once we raise the money, I'm outta here." Reese was the only person she allowed refer to her by her childhood name, *Milah*.

She banged her fist on the table, rattling the expensive cutlery. "There's always going to be something that needs doin' around here. You've been worse than Don Quixote tilting at windmills for five years. We were supposed to leave after two years…Reese."

Reese dropped his head. He felt guilty about keeping her here. For him, it had been a place to heal, but for her, it was an albatross of her own making. She should have forced his hand and said *no*. Except Reese knew her soft spots, her love for him and used them both when necessary. But she was tired of being manipulated by love and guilt.

"I am going to Sofia University with or without you. My graduate program was supposed to start in January. We paid the tuition and a deposit on an apartment. Luckily, the university gave me an extension." She waved her fork in his direction. She was impatient to live and study with creative people, to develop an identity separate from Reese Thompkins.

16

She adored him, and she needed to become a distinct human being separate from him.

"Don't do this now, Milah. There's too much going on." Reese ticked off the people still stranded here since the tornado and the deacons' refusal to accept his leadership.

Reese dug into his pocket for his ever-present antacids. She'd sat in the doctor's office when his physician forewarned him that unrelenting stress and aggravation led to ulcerative colitis. Kamilah walked to the refreshment center and held up the bottles of sparkling water and Bermuda Stone Ginger Beer. Another of her small loving touches was she anticipated most of his needs.

"Ginger Beer, please."

Kamilah brought the bottle of nonalcoholic beer to him and kissed him on the top of his head. Outside the snow continued to accumulate. It was covering the bushes, and the expansive campus was beginning to look like a beautiful winter wonderland. The snowdrifts and the falling temperatures meant canceling evening youth services. A blessing in disguise because one of the young people was hellbent on seducing the pastor.

Kamilah's words snapped at him. "Misty been callin' Genesis her mini-me and dressing her in tight, revealing clothes, and store-bought hair. Now Genesis is wearing make-up, acting like *Lolita* looking for a man to pay the bills and let her play dress-up. All of us with eyes been telling her momma she is gonna' burn in hell unless she does something soon."

"O Lord have mercy. TMI." Reese shuddered whenever forced to deal with impressionable teenage girls. Regardless of the couple's apparent love for each other, the young women at The Cathedral and a few of the seasoned saints put a bullseye on his handsome back, with Genesis being the latest. Reese had no idea how mesmerizing his eyes were or that women were attracted to powerful preachers. He was beaten down

17

from fighting with their parents, often single mothers who were unable to control their offspring's raging hormones.

Kamilah snickered, "These young folks are reading books like *Reverend Feelgood* and believe the pastor's job is to cover them." Reese fit the category of heart throb. The teens never saw him in jeans and sweatshirts. The casual knit sweaters and tailored slacks showed off his toned abs, flat stomach, and long legs. When Pastor smiled at them, his perfect white teeth gleamed.

"Which is why we encouraged you to write young adult literature." Reese was proud of the recognition Kamilah was receiving for her illustrated children's and young adult book series. "This here," he poked his chest, his island slang evident when he was under stress, "is one pastor who's not interested. If they want to play Jezebel, they can do it elsewhere. We'll even give them a letter to where they can hang out with their sisters Sapphire and Delilah."

"Stop deflecting, Reese. There's always going to be a reason to stay. But there are more compelling reasons to get the hell out of here sooner rather than later."

CHAPTER FOUR:
REESE

THE EVENING FOLLOWING THE deacon board meeting, Reese was inundated with messages from the congregation wanting to know whether the Broadcast Tower had to be replaced. Grimm and Hudson had called, emailed, and put The Cathedral's business all over social media. Most notes contained misinformation such as each member had to contribute or explain to the pastor why they were not giving. Another favorite theme was the insurance company was ready to pay out enough money to repair the Tower, but the pastor wanted something fancier. On and on and on.

Pastor Reese talked, texted, and emailed members on Sunday, Monday, and Tuesday. He assured the congregation he would discuss the project at the regular Wednesday night service. That message was a salvo to let the opposition know he was not intimidated and was proceeding with asking the congregation for support during the Wednesday evening service. Bad weather or not, church folks find a way to get to the house of God if they think a fight between the pastor and his deacons might be on the agenda.

The high-pitched ceilings of the glass atrium at the entrance to The Cathedral allowed light to shine in and enhance the access to the structure. The main auditorium resembled a performing arts center at the local community college. The sanctuary, built for congregational participation in worship, had comfortable seating, unobstructed views of the pulpit, and optimum design for sound. Behind Pastor Reese, to the left was seating for the two-hundred-fifty voice combined choirs and the musicians were arrayed on the right side. The musicians played background music as people settled in for the evening service.

Reese studied Kamilah who was seated in her customary seat in the second row of the theater style center section where she had a full visual of the raised stage. Kamilah's long hair was held away from her dark diamond-shaped face and expressive eyes with a velvet ribbon matching the cobalt-blue, lined wool slacks and muted sweater of blues and green. Her long-tapered fingers flew over her ever-present sketch pad, her oversized glasses dropping down on the bridge of her nose. She and Reese were on the same page when it came to the deacon board. Trifling.

However, if Kamilah had her way, Reese would stop fighting the deacons over every inch of progress and hand in his resignation. Today. Nothing in her smile or posture belied her exasperation with him. Milah was his anchor, the person whose approval he craved most. Yet, he'd failed to live up to his promises where she was concerned. He was caught between his own ego and his inability to step out on the faith he preached about every Sunday.

Once the members had praised, sung, and prayed, Pastor marched to the podium and stretched out his hand for quiet. "Its. Resolution. Time." His voice flowed with the drumbeat of the Congo as his long fingers waved at the four-thousand-plus members seated before him. His next statements were spoken directly to Milah and the congregation he was intent on swaying to his point of view. "Anytime God gets ready to make a move, He prepares one man. Not a mob. Not a committee. God told Abraham to go to a place He would direct him to. God commanded Noah to build the Ark. God threw Joseph in an Egyptian jail to prepare an exit strategy for his family. God dispatched Moses to Egypt. God sent Samuel to anoint David. God returned Nehemiah to Jerusalem to rebuild the wall. God sent His son Jesus to save us. And God changed Paul for him to spread the gospel."

The sanctuary was so quiet you could have heard angels weeping on the clouds. "No deacon board, no mother's board, no usher board was convened when God ordained major movements to advance His kingdom." Reese glowered down at Grimm and Hudson.

Grimm and Hudson glared back at him. If he were sticks of kindling, the altar would be a holy bonfire. Reese's beetled brows did not waver.

The organist riffed a chord. Tambourines shook. A few people stood to their feet. "Praise God for the man of God!"

Now was the time to build some bridges. Reese had a few folks on his side. "In my prayer closet, I asked God to direct me. Again, God uttered, *Rebuild the Tower*. One Godly man," Reese winked at Deacon Slay, "shared some of the congregation's concerns with me."

Deacon Slay smirked at him. *Reese remembered the conversation The two men had spent* several hours together on Tuesday when Slay urged him to slow down, ask for support, and recognize Pastor Reese was not the only one who spoke to God. Reese agreed to bring the people along rather than pushing for his vision of an immediate resolution to the Tower project.

***

The Cathedral was twenty years old. The other buildings were a gymnasium and activity center, dining hall, bookstore, dormitory-style cottages, and ten condominiums. Deacon Slay reminded the young preacher. "Pastor Winston had a vision but no money sense. Your initial infusion of personal cash kept us out of foreclosure." Deacon Slay believed in plain speaking. Discretion. Truth. Those were the things that made him the best choice for this role in this 'woodshed whippin'.' "You've done a lot of good here."

"When have I ever come to the deacon board without a concrete proposal? You know I don't deal in generalities." Reese was fighting for control of his temper. This Tower will make The Cathedral preeminent in the region. "God spoke to me; then I did my homework."

Deacon Slay snorted. "Then the Tower will be rebuilt. Who cares if it happens in the first quarter or the fourth quarter?"

21

Reese knew when to shut up and listen.

"Pastor, you're too damn impatient. You've got a big future. We know you got larger and better in you than Central Illinois." Deacon Slay's face was wreathed in smiles. "We're glad you stopped by. But ... your vision is too large for us. We a farming and retirement community with college towns like Peoria and Bloomington anchoring us. The influx of new people you are bringin' in been driving forty to fifty miles two to three times a week to worship here. We're not sure we can hold onto them when you leave."

Reese knew this dance. It would start slow and end fast. Hopefully, it would end well for both. "When y'all promoted me to the senior minister, the deacons commissioned me to grow a stagnant church. Build on the foundation Pastor Winston laid."

"You've done that. You're also a lightning rod for controversy with Grimm and Hudson." Slay grimaced, leaned back, and closed his eyes as if waiting for God to give him the words he needed. Reese noticed how frail he was. The shirt and pants were loose, the pallor showing on his brown skin. "They believe you ought to funnel the production company's profits into the church's coffers. We'd be solvent and could live off our tithes and offerings." The elder's eyes couldn't meet Reese's. The real reason for this meeting became apparent.

Reese's production company was extremely profitable. Most artists in small towns around Central Illinois didn't have access to major markets like Chicago for studio time, recording, or access to a label. Traveling back and forth to Los Angeles and New York was utterly out of their reach. With Reese's vision, secular or religious musicians could come here either to rent space or to be produced by Reese and his team. Primarily he marketed services to counties within a two-hour radius of The Cathedral and promoted to artists in Southern Illinois as an alternative to St. Louis, Missouri. The production company handled distribution of CDs and coordinated Midwest touring. The Gospel Choir was the crown jewel of the production company. The musical group was comprised of those performers who'd settled in the area after graduation from nearby universities and obtained full-time employment while pursuing singing in the evenings and on the weekends.

"Do these buffoons know anything about private ownership, separate corporations or the distinction in the laws that govern a nonprofit church and a for-profit music studio?" Lord, have these people been living under a rock? Hell no! The deacons didn't expect him to finance the church. *"The production studio was mine before I came on staff. The studio pays rent to the church for space we use whenever there's a workshop or concert. The church treasury receives all room rental and food fees. That's the music studio's only connection to the church."*

"Reese, you're coming at this with a lot of disdain for the members of the deacon board." Deacon Slay was trapped in the middle of the warring Isaac and Ishmael clans. Both sides had plausible arguments. Both sides had blind spots. *"The deacons aren't stupid. They're trying to find money and believe if you're sold out to the Lord, you should turn that production money over to help meet church expenses in this extraordinary situation."*

"If the issue is the production studio, I'll find a new location in Peoria for the studio by the end of the first quarter. With all the area foreclosures, I'm sure we can acquire new space." He'd show them how they were benefitting from the studio's location on the campus by moving it out of here… but he still owned the property the studio was erected on, not The Cathedral. Annually he paid taxes and assessments to the county.

"Stop being a petulant kid." Deacon Slay laughed, a dry sound. *"You act worse than my great grandkids when they get tapped for doin' something we told 'em not to do."*

"I'm tired of those two clowns. They want to diss my talent and my work with artists. Then, 'oh, by the way, give us the money you make wit yo' no-talent ass.'" His blood boiled. *"Hell no. They can't manage what they got on their plates."*

"Pastor, we're not goin' to scam you out of your production company. I'm old but not senile. I got a couple of grandsons who'll scam an old man quicker than Carolina Panther Cam Newton can hit long runners." Deacon Slay spent weekends watching football when he wasn't at the church. *"I brought it up so you could see what you workin against."*

"We employ a CPA to head up the church's financial team. She's the best in class. Because of the multiple entities that make up The

Cathedral, our bookkeepers and accountants keep perfect records, pay taxes on portions of income we generate from sales of books, concerts, the property we own but don't currently have a use for."

"You just don't get it, do you?"

Reese's phone chirped. He looked at it and let it go to voicemail.

"You can do everything right, and they'll still grumble and complain." Slay's voice was pacifying. "That's what they know to do."

"Deacon Slay, help me get this done."

Reese took his time, describing the damage to the Tower, the options available for restoring the structure, and his rationale for raising five million dollars. "I'm *asking*," Reese emphasized the word *asking*, "for your prayers; for your belief in spreading God's Word, and for your financial assistance to do God's work. Requesting is not the same as ordering you to support this or any other church-related project. Listen carefully so lies and half-truths won't sway you."

The members leaned forward in their plush seats. Apparently, this was not the message they were anticipating based on Twitter, Facebook, texting, and numerous telephone calls since Sunday's deacon board meeting. "God does not require you to give The Cathedral your rent or mortgage payments."

Laughter bubbled up from the pews.

"Furthermore, do not swap your utility bill money in exchange for contributing to the project."

"Amen." Deacon White said. "The utility company got all that money."

Heads nodded as members whispered and texted to both those in the house and those who couldn't make it out tonight.

This was an unexpected turn of events. No fighting in the house tonight.

"No one... not me and no church leader... is asking you to take bread out of your kids' mouths." Reese observed the audience as shoulders fell and interest shown through congregants' eyes. The room temperature returned to normal. Reese paced the pulpit area, hands in the pockets of his signature indigo robe, and stopped briefly at each of the four sections to speak directly to the members. "Before we can seek outside support, your church leadership needs two commitments from the congregation." He held up his trigger finger, "One is acceptance of why we need to rebuild."

Most heads nodded. The minority held their stiff bodies immobile since they were not willing to make any movement. Reese held up his middle finger next to the trigger finger. "The second is making... not pledging... a sacrificial gift to the project." He let that sink in for a moment.

Folks jumped to their feet. "Hallelujah. God is able! We stand on His Word."

Reese stretched out his long fingers for quiet. When the noise died down, he joked, "Y'all know I don't believe in voting. If you're for the project, please send a text or email to the church office in care of Rennett, my Director of Administration, or Tanji, the Communications Director. They, along with Rev. Thornton, will tabulate the responses. The results will be sent to Head Deacon Slay. That way, I won't be accused of tampering with the numbers."

"Amen, Pastor." Skittish laughter burst out around the sanctuary and lessened the tension of members who were ping-ponging between the pastor at the lectern and the deacons who sat together, stiff and unbending. Every time before, when the pastor asked the membership to take on a bold and audacious project, the deacon board stood with him. This public fracture was unprecedented and suggested more dissension within the church.

"Once we know the outcome, we'll take the next step." Pastor's gaze lingered briefly on each section of the church. "If you're anticipating a positive conclusion, settle it with God what manner of sacrificial gift your family can make. The gift does not have to be made today or the next week. But soon. Can we touch and agree?" Reese asked. "Stand on your feet. Sing *The Rock won't move … His Word is strong …."*

The mood was considerably lighter than when the members entered the sanctuary ninety minutes earlier. People stood, reaching for their neighbor's hand, some embracing, and a few in tears.

Deacon Grimm and Deacon Hudson walked out of the service, heads up, mouths tight, refusing to acknowledge anyone. The battle for control of The Cathedral had begun.

CHAPTER FIVE:
ZENDE

O'Hare International Airport is shut down until further notice due to a polar vortex.

WORLD-RENOWNED MUSICAL composer and performer, Zende Lightbourn listened to the recording in disbelief, then pushed Replay. The disembodied voice repeated the message.

Two weeks ago, his California-based otolaryngologist, the fancy term for doctors specializing in issues of the ear, nose, and throat, performed throat surgery to remove numerous polyps. The physician advised him against traveling for at least thirty days, but Zende was restless. As part of his bi-coastal career, he owned a beach house with an in-home studio in LA, performed at "It" spots and enjoyed a fair amount of celebrity. However, his primary residence was in Boston where he worked with a few students from the Berklee School of Music. Very few of his fans knew his parents' dream for him was performing classical music. Although he couldn't sing, he could work on his next commissioned project in his home's state-of-the-art music studio. He could sit in with the Berklee Symphony whenever he desired. The Symphony was a fantastic place to rekindle the excitement he'd once had for his career.

On Saturday, Zende direct flight from Los Angeles to Boston had an engine malfunction, and the plane was diverted to O'Hare. He was rescheduled to depart for Boston at 10:00

a.m. on Sunday. He checked into the presidential suite at the W Hotel for one night. The snowstorm hit in the wee hours of Sunday morning, dumping twenty-four feet of snow in Boston and the surrounding area. Today was Friday; snow was still clogging traffic arteries across the Midwest and East coast. His throat burned worse than eating habanero peppers within hours of having a tonsillectomy. Absently he reached for the throat spray and took a couple of quick puffs. The medication did little to alleviate the burning pain.

Zende showered, dressed, and ordered room service to bring up a smoothie and herbal tea. These damn restrictions were frustrating his life. He couldn't drink alcohol until his throat healed. He'd barely slept this week. Memories of his muse's face, scent, and laughter he usually kept at bay deluged him and haunted his dreams. But life was not a golf game or a music score where second chances happened all the time. But he could atone for being an asshole.

He'd picked up the phone on numerous occasions, punched in the digits, backpedaled, and hung up. Zende was self-centered. He wanted an everlasting relationship to duplicate the loving marriage his parents shared. He hadn't counted on interference or his own miscalculations pushing his lover into making another choice. He desperately desired a do-over.

His muscles screamed for a hot stone massage. He dialed the concierge and asked for the first available ninety-minute massage.

"Will there be anything else, Mr. Lightbourn?"

"Nothing." He disconnected.

The skilled masseuse earned the tip for beating the kinks out of Zende's shoulders and back. The frustrated musician opened his composition app, doodled for forty-five minutes, saved his work, and strode over to look out the window at the wind gusts and tiny people scurrying around on the packed snow and ice. The one person he desperately desired was at least three hours away. His dropping in after five years of crickets would be disruptive, and he wouldn't be welcomed like the prodigal son. Zende was tired of his own company and didn't want to spend Friday night with a group of local musicians when he was unable to participate in the jam session. He shrugged off the gloomy thoughts. Zende pulled out his phone, found the name and number for one of his Brown University classmates who lived in the Windy City and punched the button.

***

His "date" refused to travel downtown because of the weather. Because of the city's inadequate snow removal system on side streets in the neighborhoods and limited parking, Noori suggested Zende hire a town car to drop him off at Hyde Park's A10 Restaurant and return later. With an extensive menu and specialty drinks, the dining establishment was bursting with guests feening for music and alcoholic drinks after being cooped up all week. Zende's shoulders dropped at least two inches as the restaurant's ambiance and Chicago's famous house music kicked in.

Zende relaxed in the leather seat, raised his mug of tea, and extended it to his companion. "Dr. Annorah Sherman...other than that bruise, you are sho nuff looking prosperous." He pointed to her eye like a conductor singling out an out-of-tune instrument. Her boots added several inches to her height. Her hair was done up in recently styled micro braids. She wore a cherry-tomato colored Ellen Tracy pantsuit and a full-length black ranch mink coat with matching hat and gloves. Refusing the hostess' offer to hang up her outer garment, Noori insisted the fur remain on the seat next to her.

Noori snickered and clinked her Long Island Iced Tea glass with his hot beverage. "After too many cocktails on New

Year's Eve, I slipped on some ice outside my building." She rubbed the discolored skin. Noori tittered and changed the subject. "I stream all your albums and singles."

"Glad to hear it." Zende could care less about record sales. For all his celebrity, music took a back seat to figuring out how to change his personal situation. "The industry competition is fierce. If you aren't innovating, a fresh face or a new interpretation of an old master will replace you." By the time his throat healed, he'd better be ready to drop several projects consecutively.

Noori knocked back her Long Island Iced Tea. Catching the eye of one of the two African bartenders, she signaled for another one. "The real world is brutal. Once upon a time, we considered the cruelest punishment was being stuck in one of Rhode Island's snowstorms." Her hand reached for the munchies, spilling a few onto the high gloss wooden table.

He nodded. "As a kid, I spun the globe and swore I'd get to Rhode Island to discover my heritage. My mother's Native American ancestors lived in the area before being sold and shipped to Bermuda."

"When you weren't playing gigs up and down the eastern seaboard, you were rummaging through old musty records in the genealogy library," Noori reminded him, leaning back in her chair and waving at a couple of people standing at the hostess's desk.

After graduation, he moved to Boston while refining his sound, playing gigs with various regional groups until he acquired a reputation and a following. Once he attained a name and wealth on the East Coast, he was invited to LA to compose music for several projects.

This place was filling up fast. Zende eye-hustled a good-looking woman holding court with a group of women at the end of the bar. Drinks were flowing. The women danced with each other. He assumed she was the stud. About five-ten, she was wearing a man-tailored black suit and short black boots.

Her curly hair was styled in a distinctively fashionable male haircut. She wore several diamond rings on her fingers.

Another African waiter took their food order. Zende ordered a salad, hearty soup, and a banana split soft serve for dessert. Noori ordered a spinach and feta pizza. The first waiter scurried over with Noori's second drink. He addressed her professionally. "Dr. Sherman, Lyn sent this drink to you, miss. She said to tell you 'Happy New Year'."

Noori whipped her head around to the bar where the stud lifted her long-necked bottle of imported beer and saluted her. Noori rolled her eyes.

"To each his own." Zende laughed.

Noori shuddered. "Not what you're thinking. We're in the same homeowner's association."

Fifteen minutes later, one of the servers set their selections in front of them. "Anything else, sir… miss?"

"Thanks, nothing for me." Zende picked up on the young man's formal speech. They were either Nigerian students or immigrants. "What about you, Noori?"

"You can't mess up pizza." The petulant princess barely acknowledged the wait staff.

Zende didn't remember Noori being this brittle in college or the few times he'd seen her socially since then. He was too starved to care. They ate in silence with only the chatter from other diners, clinking glasses, and waiters clearing tables. After his initial hunger was sated, Zende changed the subject. "Tell me what a behavioral psychologist does?"

"We deal with sexual dysfunction and alternative lifestyles along with the usual psychotics in clinic settings." She threw her hand up, dismissively. "In research, we're examining trends associated with dysfunctional lifestyles and their impact on social policy."

Her body language confused him. How do you spend ten to twelve years preparing for a career and then act like the people you swore to heal are beneath you? "What happened to treating depression, bipolar disorders, and counseling families?"

"Those issues are relegated to the background or to clinicians who earned degrees through some of these online universities. Nobody cares about bulimia or anorexia when Dr. Phil and talk show hosts are "treating," she crooked her fingers, "them so miserably."

Zende gawked at her dismissal of people's issues. "Is there any part of the job you enjoy?"

"I set the social policy agenda, which gets my juices flowing." Noori pushed the pizza around the plate, nibbling on the cheese and the crust. "I don't have to listen to the excuses, the distasteful stories, or worry about who the patients might harm next."

"Since the field has become so objectionable, why keep working in it?" Zende couldn't conceive of being in a career he found unpleasant or unsatisfying. He loved the ins and outs of the music industry. The house music playing in the background had him wishing he'd opted for the jam session after all.

"The job pays the bills. My lifestyle is not cheap." Noori stopped eating and pushed the pizza away. She leaned in and placed her hands on the table. "I love to travel on the organization's dime."

Deciding he didn't care enough to pursue it, Zende checked out the gold encrusted band on her left hand. "Got anybody in particular who takes your mind off work and gives you a different perspective?" His gaze wandered back to Lyn with a woman draped over her arm.

"I was married for a short time. What a loser." Noori tossed back the rest of her drink and signaled for a third drink. "After Dolton, I stopped listening to my parents' opinions about men."

The waiter set her drink down and left without any acknowledgment from her.

Zende envied his parents' spiritual connection and refused to settle for less. He'd almost forgotten where his heart was until he asked the wrong woman to wear his ring and she'd insisted he set a wedding date. "You had no idea of who he was before you married him?"

"Dolton Simmons had the right pedigree." Noori ticked them off one by one. "We'd known each other since infancy. Family name. Money. Two degrees from Harvard. Duller than dirt. On high school prom night, my dad scared Dolton to death with his little 'You bring my daughter back like you found her' speech."

Zende's raspy laughter caused other diners, as well as Lyn, to turn and stare at them. He raised a hand to their waiter. "Please bring me a cola."

The waiter hurried over with the soft drink.

"Thanks." Zende handed him a huge tip.

"My dad selected him. I accepted it." Noori sniffed as though she found the decision distasteful. "Y'all say men know how to handle their business in bed. He didn't."

"And you couldn't tell him or show him what you needed?" This was jacked up. He didn't usually talk about sex with women unless he was planning to bed them.

Noori looked him up and down as though he was one of his Algonquin relatives on the slave block in Barr's Bay, Bermuda and asked, "You in a relationship?" She picked up her drink.

"Same old Noori." In your face and pushing the boundaries of politeness while keeping you out of her business. "Nope. Never married."

"Whatever happened to the girl from Bermuda? Did she get fat, marry someone else, and pop out a bunch of babies while you were at Brown?" Noori would not have made a

33

politician or police investigator. No subtlety. She went straight for the juggler when she was unsure of her footing.

"We lost track of each other." This impromptu dinner meeting hadn't been such a good idea. He could have found lighter conversation eating at the W's piano bar. "Why do you even care?"

"Recently, an article about a woman who's making a name for herself writing kids' books caught my eye."

"Lots of people write children's books." Zende couldn't follow the twists and jumps in the conversation. Noori was probably miserable she'd shared something so personal, so she was turning the tables on him.

"She illustrates stories for kids living in nontraditional families." Noori acted as if her commentary was noteworthy.

"Probably not something I'd pick up."

"Something about her face reminded me of a picture you kept on your desk at Brown."

"I can't remember half the people I attended classes with for four years, and you remember a girl we talked about maybe once over a dozen years ago."

"Probably my overactive imagination."

Zende lost his appetite for the delicious food and her company. People-watching at the W was more fun than this. He signaled the waiter for the bill. "What's the name of the magazine? I'll get a copy and test your powers of recall."

The waiter rushed over with the bill. Zende glanced at the total and pulled out enough bills to cover it along with an extra generous tip to make up for Noori's rudeness.

"I kept the magazine. Although the article was vague, it might come in handy one day for the Institute's research agenda." She stood up without giving him a chance to help her with her chair or the coat. "Walk me home. Your car can pick you up there."

.

CHAPTER SIX: KAMILAH

FOR THE SENIOR PASTOR'S residence, Rev. Winston built the Winston House: seven thousand square feet of stone, marble, and glass palace to wine and dine prospective donors. The oversized rooms flowed into one another, large bedrooms, sitting rooms, a small theatre, offices, and a chapel making this an event planner's dream home. The commercial kitchen contained one wall of stainless-steel appliances, miles of countertops, a center island for prep work including cooktop and sink. The second island was used to set up food before serving. Situated in one wing of the Winston House showpiece was a sizeable three-bedroom apartment where Reese and Kamilah Thompkins resided instead of occupying the entire home.

Kamilah redecorated their private wing with touches from Bermuda. The textiles and furniture were designed by her classmates at SCAD, Savannah College of Art and Design. Bright colors—melon, orange, crimson, turquoise, and ocean blue added cheerfulness to the pale blue-gray walls. The wall art was a mixture of her own paintings as well as numerous craftsmen she'd met on their travels to Europe and Africa. The third and largest bedroom was transformed into her private design studio because of its cathedral ceiling and skylight. As lovely as this apartment was, it belonged to The Cathedral, and when this skirmish between Reese and the deacons blew up, similarly to Israel and Palestine in the fight over the Gaza strip, she and Reese would be homeless.

Currently, the underutilized Winston House was the site used to host parties for the large groups who came for the weekend and occasionally week-long spiritual retreats and team building. Kamilah eyed the approximately fifty adolescents milling around the open space and smothered a laugh. A Decatur, Illinois youth group scheduled this weekend sleep-over at The Cathedral last fall, never dreaming minus twelve-degree temperatures would close the region down for most of the week. The church leaders braved the eighty miles of bad roads to bring the teens anyway.

Grace Winston, Youth Director, had served as her widowed father's hostess at the Winston House. She earned a Master of Divinity Degree with additional studies in youth development and pastoral care. Fortyish, with her trim figure and white spiked hair, Grace coordinated programming for the various youth groups who frequented their facilities and remained a vital part of the overall ministries. Grace organized the joint choir rehearsal as a natural icebreaker which allowed the Decatur adolescents to get acquainted with The Cathedral's youth group. Pastor Reese promised to record the three best groups during the Saturday evening service.

Following choir rehearsal, The Cathedral's young people served a dinner of subs, potato salad, and chips for their guests. Some of the younger married couples and the adult supervisors from Decatur, spent more time getting acquainted with each other than circulating among the teenagers who'd staked out three areas of the room: the food table, the dance floor and small conversation hubs. Milah placed these young people in hypothetical groups. The truly anointed were moving among their guests, seeking to be of service to God and others. The Devils-In-Training had absorbed too much of the secular world and were vying for attention. Those straddling both worlds, wanting the popularity but not ready to cross any lines, circled the other two groups.

Kamilah needed a third eye to watch these kids and keep track of Miss Genesis who was wearing too much make-up, dressed in body-constricting red ski pants and a closer-fitting sweater showing off her ample breasts. Feet encased in brown suede UGGs fairly flew around the dance floor with her freshly braided hair whipping around.

"Pastor Reese, we wanna show you the latest dance moves." Genesis swiveled her hips. Kamilah's heart and soul ached for Reese. He and the ministry staff were battered from a week of church skirmishes, assisting stranded motorists, and ensuring The Cathedral's ground crew was plowing and shoveling for families living around them, regardless of age or economic status. Over dinner, Genesis and her little gang were all over Pastor Reese, asking questions and interrupting grown folks' conversations.

"Can we sing with 'cha, Pastor? Show these kids we got it goin' on." Tayshaun, her BFF, held up her hand as if it were a microphone.

Reese's body sagged a little as he excused himself from the kids and maneuvered away before getting frustrated. He whispered to Kamilah, "I'm going to take a long, hot shower and work on my sermon for a while." He kissed her briefly. "Being around these young people furnishes me some insight about bringing unloved, unchurched and unwanted children into God's kingdom."

Reese hadn't been gone twenty minutes when Kamilah's antenna went on high alert. "Grace, where's Genesis?" Kamilah asked the woman responsible for chaperoning the rambunctious teens.

Grace looked in each of the four corners of the humongous room. "I'll find her." Grace searched the bathrooms and lesser used spaces for the girl. No Genesis.

Kamilah raced down the hall and entered her apartment when they couldn't find her in the public spaces. As soon as she came into the suite, Kamilah heard the shower running. She followed the sounds.

Genesis was standing outside the bathroom. Her hand was on the doorknob.

Kamilah yelled at the girl. "Young lady, what are you doing here?" Kamilah wanted to snatch Genesis' sewn-in braids and slap some sense into her.

Startled, Genesis' neck rocked, but it lacked any fire. She mumbled, "I got my period."

"And there weren't enough stalls in the public bathrooms?" Genesis had missed the whole point of the purity classes: modesty, wisdom, and high personal standards.

Genesis avoided Kamilah's stare and mumbled, "I ... needed some privacy."

Kamilah grabbed Genesis by her arm and drug her down the hall into the living room. "Sit down!" She sucked in air to quiet her chaotic thoughts. "How did you get past a locked door?"

Genesis sat on the couch, head down, refusing to meet the older woman's stare. "The music director was talkin' with Pastor... and I kind a slipped in."

Kamilah sat next to the lying teen, her leg throbbing from the intense cold and the amount of time she'd spent trailing behind teenagers today. "Girl, why do you come to church?"

Crocodile tears spurted from Genesis' eyes. "You're mean." Genesis attempted to get up.

Kamilah pulled her back down. She pinched the bridge of her own nose instead of gripping the girl's upper arm the way Mommy used to do when she caught Milah lying. "Pastor left. You went ghost. You want to run that by me again."

Genesis jerked.

***

Just this past Sunday, he'd ended their meditation with, "We have to do something about Genesis Hardeman." His island dialect resurfaced in times of extreme distress.

"What's she done now?" Raised in a home with a single mother and without a man in the house, the girl was curious about male-female interactions and how to get her own man. The girl turned sixteen and declared her number one goal in life was to sleep with the senior pastor. No amount of scolding, counseling or punishment had discouraged her so far.

"I walked into the office. The young heifer's open legs were draped across the chair arms, rooting' around in my chair without any panties on. Her honey pot was glistening and drippin' for anyone to see." Pastor Reese drug his weary hand down his face as he tried to contain the bile she knew was roiling in his already acidic stomach. "What if one of our members or donors, expecting to see me had walked in and found her." Reese shuddered. "They could have misread the situation and wreaked havoc on me."

"**I**t's going to get a lot more unpleasant if you don't tell me why you're prowling around in my private space." The older woman tilted Genesis' chin up, forcing the girl to look her in the eyes. "You have one minute. Either I call your mother, or I call the po-po and have you arrested for trespassing."

"A credit card." Genesis barely moved her lips and dug her feet into the thick carpet.

"Huh?"

"I used a credit card to jimmy the lock." Genesis' voice was barely audible.

Kamilah often dealt with rebellion, anger, and hostility. To see all three wrapped up in this sixteen-year-old was a lethal combination. "Call your mother."

***

Kamilah and Grace stashed Genesis in Pastor Winston's former office while they waited for Misty to arrive. The workspace had the musty smell of unused space. Reese kept the bulk of his correspondence in their apartment or at the studio. Genesis was huddled on the couch and sniffling when her mother ran in.

"Genesis." Misty Hardeman sprinted into the office and snatched her daughter by the front of her sweater. "Stop acting like you ain't had no home training." Misty lacked parenting skills. She bought clothes, gave Genesis too much allowance and engaged in inappropriate conversations with the girl.

Genesis rolled her eyes and flung her hands out like the drama queen she was. "I'm not like these stupid little girls you want me to hang out with." Next, she'd be stamping her feet or having a temper tantrum. "I'm gonna have his baby."

"Stop chasing a married man." Misty's eyes begged for support from Kamilah and Grace.

Her mother's indecisiveness stoked Genesis' fury. "You always tellin' yo girlfriends how you slept with my pops and he had a wife at the time. You were bragging—"

Misty's hand whipped out like lightning, leaving a palm print on Genesis' mocha face.

Kamilah started forward.

Grace grabbed her arm and mouthed, "They need to work this out."

Misty tossed her long curly weave out of her face. "Yo pops ran back to his wife and their three kids." The barely forty-year-old single mother acted like she was going to pull out some Vaseline and a can of whoop ass. "Has Pastor Reese ever shown the slightest interest in you?"

Genesis howled, backing away from her mother. "No."

"Touched you?" Misty pushed three fingers into Genesis' chest.

"Un un." Genesis whimpered, tears streaming down her face. She rubbed at the red handprints marring her cheek.

"Emailed you?" Misty was relentless.

"Nope." Genesis turned wet, pleading eyes toward Kamilah and Grace.

Kamilah placed a wad of tissues in Genesis' hands to wipe her face and snotty nose. The girl was being humiliated by her mother. As much as Kamilah wanted to spank Genesis, this was not a good idea. Kamilah reached out a hand to Misty, whose body was shaking violently. The woman ignored her.

Mother was face-to-nose with the daughter. "What the hell is wrong with you, Genesis?"

These were the pain-filled words of a woman refusing to let her daughter follow in her shallow footsteps. Misty was trying to stop a train wreck. The Bible talks about the sins of the father visited on the children. But no one talks about the sins of the mother coming back to bite her in the ass.

Genesis mumbled through her misery. "... searched out a woman and she gave me potions to make him fall in love with me."

"Who ... what ... when?" Misty got up in Genesis' face again.

Grace pulled Misty back this time.

Genesis' big eyes focused on her mother. "When we flew to New Orleans for the Bayou Classic at Thanksgiving, I took a picture of Pastor Reese to a woman with second sight. She said it was gonna happen."

The three women looked at each other like Satan had walked in and taken center stage.

"Get pregnant." Genesis talked to Misty like trying to make a child understand washing their hands after using the toilet.

"Were you planning to drug a married man and have sex with him?" Misty screeched.

Kamilah threaded her hands through her hair to keep from slapping the taste out of Genesis' mouth. Nothing in her education or experience matched up with this girl's confusion about what it meant to be a woman.

Grace separated mother and child, moving her hands up and down Misty's back. She fixed her somber gaze on Genesis. "Sit down, Genesis."

Kamilah massaged her temples and gritted her teeth. This nightmare had been building for months. No matter how many times she'd warned Reese or Grace that they were dealing with more than teenage angst, neither had taken her seriously until Reese saw her rooting around in his office chair.

"Genesis, you're better than this." Misty sat down next to her wayward daughter. She grabbed Genesis' hands, letting the tears fall on her daughter's hands. "I don't regret having you. Every time Myra crosses my path, I'm thankful she's a God-fearing woman. She hates my ass, but Myra made sure Frank took care of you." Misty frowned, relaxing her grip on the squirming girl child. "When he was out of a job, Myra paid the child support and insurance out of her pocket."

Kamilah stepped in. She didn't want to know another word of this family's business. "Listen to your momma, Genesis. Stop chasing behind Pastor Reese."

Her lips trembling, Genesis nodded.

Kamilah touched Misty's shoulder, finding it tight as a guitar string. "Pastor Reese has enough responsibilities without your daughter trying to destroy his ministry." Misty was on notice and would have to deal with her daughter.

Misty had to have the last word. "Little girl. Let me tell you something on the real. Do this again, and I'll stomp yo ass like wine growers smashing their grapes. Do you understand?"

"Yes, ma'am." Genesis was cowed, but this scrimmage with her mother wasn't over.

Misty rolled her eyes. "You owe the pastor an apology and a new chair. Sister Kamilah, send us a bill. Genesis will empty out her Christmas money as soon as the banks open."

CHAPTER SEVEN: REESE

EARLY THE NEXT MORNING, Reese drove one of the neon green and blue snowmobiles over the sprawling twenty-five-hundred-acre complex to the production studio, hoping to sort out his personal and prophetic issues. He and Kamilah had rehashed the Genesis mess. Reese's focus must be on rebuilding God's Tower and then resigning. Reese could leave with Kamilah or deal with the fallout when she didn't return. The tone of Kamilah's voice and the set of her mouth convinced him she would enroll in the summer session at Sofia University with or without him. It seemed Deepak Chopra was teaching a summer seminar on mind-body balance. She intended to be sitting in the front row.

Once out of his warm jacket and brewing coffee in the Keurig, Reese had the production house to himself. There weren't any performers brave enough to tackle the snow-packed roads. Being outside in the frigid air had reinvigorated his brain cells and sparked Reese's creative juices. Maybe, if he put down some tracks, and wrote a couple of tunes, his sober self could clarify how to serve God and give Kamilah the freedom she desperately needed.

He chose one of the smaller studios in the state-of-the-art facility. Reese laid tracks for hours, losing track of time. His brain created music incorporating the whistling wind, the laughter of kids as they played in impressive mountains of white powder. His concentration waned as he finished the rhythm section by coordinating the sounds of kids sliding down man-made snow hills and their laughter with snowplows moving mounds of dirty white snow from highways. He scrubbed at his gritty eyes with the heels of his hands. When he reopened the tired orbs, he was squinting into the face of a ghost.

Shortly after his parents' death, Reese had been hanging out by himself. He couldn't remember where Milah and the others were. He needed to go to the bathroom. Right now! He couldn't make it home without pissing himself. He didn't dare go in the men's restroom without a look-out. So, he waited and watched until the coast was clear and raced into the women's restroom. He finished, washed his hands, and checked to see if the coast was clear. A couple of steps away from safety, American accents slurred "a dude's comin' out of the women's toilet."

Trapped. Reese's eyes darted around the dark alley, and for a millisecond, he saw an escape hatch. Before he could slip through, one of the men grabbed him from behind. His worst nightmare. Alone. Unable to get to the knife he kept in a sheath strapped to his ankle.

"Check the bathroom. This fag could be a rapist or a murderer."

"We'll be heroes." Another high pitched voice.

The guy who grabbed him pulled the back of his old cotton shirt ready for the rag bag. The ripping sound terrified him.

"Man, this a damn tranny!" Island visitors. Drunk. "We need to teach this he-she a lesson." He shook Reese like a rag doll without the stuffing, "I gotta sister and perverts like you got no business using the same bathroom."

"A damn abomination 'for God. Kick his ass."

Reese fought, struggling to get to the knife, kicking out, outnumbered three to one and outmuscled. He was tossed around as they tore at his clothes, blackened both his eyes, and punched him repeatedly in his ribs. One of them threw him on the hard ground. He curled into a fetal ball, unable to stop them, letting the pain take him over. One of the guys yanked his pants off.

"Get the hell away from him." Two men waded into the fight, punching the most massive bigot in the stomach. His companion grabbed the one pulling at Reese's clothes and landed a couple of vicious kicks to the man's groin. The three ruffians got in several brutal punches to his back before running off.

An island voice sounded close to his ear. "Are you okay?" The men were kneeling on both sides of him, gingerly touching his battered body.

45

Mute, he shook his head until he was able to open one eye to a slit.

"Reese, damn it. Is that you?" Zende's hands touched the battered face, reached into his pocket for a handkerchief and tried to wipe away some of the blood pouring from the younger boy's nose and mouth.

With the buzzing in his ears, tears clogging his throat, and the searing pain in his gut, Reese struggled to his knees and fell back screaming in agony. He wanted to vomit, to crawl into a hole and die.

"Reese! Man, it's Zende."

The familiar voice penetrated the pain, the terror and offered him a lifeline. Zende: his savior and his lifesaver. Reese sank back to the ground and wept. The vicious beating, the ugly words. Those men ripping at his clothes and shouting obscenities. They intended to rape and or kill him. "Please... get me outta here 'fore they come back."

Zende took off his shirt, put it on Reese, and buttoned up the front. Zende and his friend held up Reese's light weight between them, dragging him to Zende's car where they put him in the back seat of the Toyota Four by Four. "You need a doctor."

"No ... no doctor. Take me to the theater... somebody ... help me."

And they did. Reese's ribs were bruised, not broken. The male performers taped him up, put salve on his eyes, doped him up with somebody else's pain pills, and made up a bed for him to sleep on. He stayed in bed for a week with Milah hovering around as much as she could get away from their guardian, Tootie.

Over the next month, the pain receded as the bruises turned purple and black. Reese could breathe again without coughing. He declared, "Never again." He'd piss his pants before going to a restroom without a lookout. Furthermore, he would find a way to have the trans surgery, to be anatomically a man and living as he was preordained.

Reese's heart moved from his throat back to its usual place as he followed Zende's eyes checking out the equipment and the setup. Growing up in Bermuda, Zende and Reese, the two best young musicians and competitors had been mentored by Chris, 'the piano man'. The boys played a game of one-upmanship. Outdoing each other vocally or on the instruments was the highlight of their days. Only when the lights went up on stage did they remember why they were a team. Zende sang baritone to Reese's tenor.

"That's gonna be one intense song." Zende sauntered into the studio door, holding the Canadian Goose snow jacket over his arm, a black watch cap pulled snug over his dreadlocks.

Reese resumed blending sounds, his head moving in rhythm with the beat in his head. "I heard the music this morning. It was vital to lay it down before the worries of the day pushed the notes aside. The words will come later."

"Man, this rivals any studio in LA or Boston." Zende enthused as he checked out the equipment.

Reese accepted the high praise from the consummate musician who also played several instruments. Reese followed Zende's career of composing and directing shows for big-name performers and his solo albums.

Zende tapped his chin with his finger. "you're not what I expected."

Reese saved his work, shut down the machine, and faced the man who'd once saved his life, yet didn't understand why it was necessary to assist him. "What the hell does that mean? That I got out of Bermuda and went to university. That I became educated instead of a sideshow freak. That I learned God loves me."

Reese beckoned Zende to come in and to sit at the table across from him. "What trade wind blew you over here, Zende? Last we knew you were at the Sundance Film Festival, engaged to marry some black American princess whose broke father saw you as a cash cow or a stud. Either way, they'd have you on the short leash for a lifetime."

Zende laughed, "You got a piece of the tale and embroidered the rest. My fiancée and I parted on amicable terms. There's only one woman I'm interested in spending my life with."

"Took you long enough to figure it out. You came all this way for nothing." Reese's left hand played a nasty riff on the keyboard. "She's no longer interested in you."

"We had interference." Zende spoke through clenched teeth. "You had an agenda and a strong influence on her. I've matured, and I'm not leavin without my woman this time."

"Are your parents going to accept her this time? Can they stomach the thought of you marrying a woman with a trans brother?" Reese lifted his head and ceased fiddling with the keyboard to assess the tense vibrations rolling off Zende. Zende Lightbourn's family was island royalty. Zende's father was a high-ranking official of the Progressive Labour Party. His mother was a descendant of the Algonquin Native Americans who were banished to Bermuda in the 1700s by the New England colonists and sold into slavery after the Pequot War. A British officer married the Algonquin maiden and produced many children.

"Reese, don't mess this up again." Zende's tone was calm and deliberate. Reese had rarely seen the man since he left Bermuda for Brown University. Zende and Kamilah drifted apart because Zende's dual focus was on his music and researching his Algonquin heritage. The Lightbourn family wanted him to pursue a classical music career, but the talented musician was determined to do his own thing.

Reese lifted his head to assess the tense vibrations rolling off Zende and the meaning behind the words. He'd been grateful when Zende disappeared from both their lives. The actual physical transition from female to male had been long and difficult. Doctors prescribed drugs. Psychoanalysis. Dealing with hateful people at every turn. Only sheer will and Kamila had gotten him through. "What's your plan? I know you got one."

"Why would I tell you? So, you can make a mess of things again."

"She's my sister." Zende wanted to separate him and Kamilah, take her so far away that the connection between the two of them no longer existed. All his life, Kamilah had been the one fighting beside him against the slights, the taunts, the bullies. When he'd cry at night, she let him crawl into bed with her; she say, "don't worry. We go you. We won't ever let them win."

"Don't you mean she's your 'pretend wife'? Don't you mean she's your shield against the truth?"

Reese gritted his teeth. "Who's delusional now? You drop in, in the middle of a snowstorm and start making demands. My life as a trans man is none of yo business."

Zende wandered over to a wall covered with news articles, awards, platinum albums, pictures of Reese with the Gospel Choir, even a couple of scenes including Kamilah. "I was stuck in Chicago during the airport's inability to remove the snow and get me home. I decided we needed a come-to-Jesus meeting... a long-overdue conversation."

"What you talkin' 'bout?"

Zende's anger laced the words, "... man, you're a fraud. A straight up blasphemer. I don't have a clue how you defrauded these people all these years. You don't even look the same."

Neither Reese nor Kamilah had seen or talked to Zende in years. Not a Christmas card or a birthday greeting. It was as if the two musicians had an unspoken pact to keep their professional distance. At least Reese did. "My flock will tell you I'm preaching, teaching and leading lost souls to Christ."

"And perpetrating a fraud. Lying by omission. Zende pointed to a picture of Reese in a Ralph Lauren suit. The face was angular, more masculine. Listening intently, he realized Reese's vocals had deepened. "They'd throw yo ass out of here so fast, you'd probably land somewhere across the pond in England." Zende's frustrated, angry fists pounded on the table.

His voice rose, "You were resourceful but broke, Reese, when you left Bermuda to attend university. How'd you come by the kind of money necessary for the physical enhancements and to create this setup?"

Reese plastered on a fake smile. "One of Chris' benefactors awarded me a music scholarship to enroll in Bradley University. In the months before classes started, I wandered around, getting oriented and finding a place to live comfortably without a lot of nosy neighbors or other students around. During my explorations of the area, I kept hearing about these gospel choirs at five or six colleges and universities in the Central Illinois region and decided to check them out. Man, they were talented but at different stages and with unique struggles."

Zende mulled the words over in his brain, pacing back and forth, taking in more of the set-up. He shook his head in disbelief at both the physical changes in Reese as well as the while growing up in the place, he must have absorbed every facet of the Bermuda theatre world.

"They were small, disconnected and had no vision. I met with the directors, sat in on rehearsals and shared my belief the choirs collective strength lay in coming together to improve their range and become more visible. I decided to make it happen by hosting the first ever Central Illinois Christmas cantata using my share of the settlement money the cruise ship paid out when our parents drowned.

During the fall semester, while engaged with full-time studies, I rearranged pieces of holiday music, added a little island flava' and taught them to each choir. The three weekends preceding Thanksgiving, the six choirs came together at the Bone Student Center at Illinois State University. Collectively, they shaped an incredible arrangement transforming traditional Christmas music into an expression of highest praise, joy, and wonderment. The cantata was held the first weekend in December to three sold-out crowds. We videoed, audiotaped, and digitally mastered CDs and videotapes. We mailed pre-paid tapes out in time for Christmas. I paid the expenses, kept fifty percent of the profits for future projects, and distributed the rest to the participating choirs."

Zende nodded his head in amazement. "Sharing the money with the groups was a stroke of genius."

Reese shrugged. "I learned from the shadiest con artists on the island. Artists who blew up while the backup singers remained broke boys and girls in the Lord. When the CD was released, I received requests from promoters and sponsors wanting in on upcoming events. I declined most of them. My long-term personal goal was to grow the group into a cohesive paid group."

Zende taunted him. "Why settle for a production company instead of public notoriety? You got the pretty boy look. We know you can sing and play with the elite musicians anywhere."

Reese ignored the insult. "My gospel collaborations grew from that initial success. My theological studies expanded my biblical knowledge, compared Christianity with world religions, and helped me to refine my belief system. Someone nicknamed me *Pastor Reese*, and it stuck. Pretty soon, it was real."

Four years after that first cantata, Pastor Reese had developed a name, a strong following, several CDs, records climbing up the charts and offers to appear across the Midwest. "Singing and managing a group of college students was not my long-range goal. I was approached by promoters with a lot of big talk about moving up to the big time. Money was made in the front office, production, promotion, mixing it up, wheeling and dealing. You've seen the write-ups and heard the music. We've been nominated for a Stellar Award."

"All the while playing your greatest theatrical role." Zende's voice oozed sarcasm.

"Telling the truth." Reese knew Zende was spoiling for a fight. "My ministry is about trying to humanize this experience.

I'm tired of people havin' to wait for paradise after death. They can encounter heaven right here on earth."

"With you as the master teacher?" Zende snapped his fingers in Reese's direction.

Reese didn't accept disrespect about the choices he'd made. The past thirteen years had been profitable. He hadn't taken a vow of poverty like the priests and nuns who begged tourists for money to provide modest school improvements for their students. "Books, speaking fees, contributions and consultations are part of my income." He'd used part of the money to pay for the surgery.

"How long are you going to run this scam on these people?" Zende inhaled deep breaths. He held up his hands in the symbol of peace. "Kamilah's leaving is going to reveal you, either as a man who can't hang on to his woman or a fraud. Right now, Kamilah runs interference from the women who think you are so hot."

"Zende, you came here to tell me you are stealing Milah." Reese steepled his hands and quieted his pounding heart. "You always were a self-centered ass. You have no idea of who I am." Reese had to bend, if only for Milah's benefit. "Go. Talk to her. Ask her what she wants to do."

CHAPTER EIGHT: KAMILAH

KAMILAH STARED AT ZENDE as if he were an apparition. Her vision blurred; her heart thudded as if it wanted to jump out of her chest. Her chest seized up. *God, you got jokes.*

They'd been intimate for the first time the night before Zende left for his freshman year at Brown University, shortly after he'd rescued Reese from the thugs in St. George's. On that starry night aboard his father's boat, they drank champagne, ate shrimp, oysters, and fish dripping with butter, licking the crumbs off each other until their hunger blazed for each other instead of food. To Zende's delight, Kamilah was a virgin. Island girls were often mothers before they graduated high school. But not his Milah. They pledged their undying love and the next morning, he dropped her off at her guardian's home before heading to L.F. Wade International Airport for his flight to Providence, Rhode Island.

***

She'd stopped praying for his return years ago. Six years ago, when Reese initially begged her to accompany him to Serbia for gender reassignment surgery, she prayed Zende would rescue her from herself. She was too proud to contact him on her own. Ultimately, her love for Reese led her into this deception. Regardless of the terms: two years and done they agreed to, she was still playacting as First Lady. When Zende called off his engagement eighteen months ago, he'd made no attempt to contact her. Kamilah concluded he was moving on with his life. She was determined to do the same and began researching graduate school programs. No more standing on the sidelines wishing and dreaming.

Kamilah invited her former lover into her private office off the lobby of The Cathedral and offered him a seat at her crowded worktable. Zende's gaze traveled around the office she'd decorated with Bermuda seascapes and landmarks recreated from memory, overflowing bookshelves, and sketchbooks on the roundtable. Emotions warred between anger and precious childhood memories as she sat across from Zende of the thick lashes, almond-shaped eyes, square jawline, high cheekbones, and full mouth. His presence reminded her of sun-washed days, blue skies, the ocean, and women whose hips swayed to old Caribbean drumbeats. The mingled sounds of Africa, South America and Europe twisted and tangled on the tongues of Islanders and visitors alike. But she remembered how he'd made love to her, left, and broke his numerous promises to come back for her.

"I came to apologize, to make amends." Zende's baritone was raspy, his handsome face pale with dark circles under his eyes.

He reached for her hands; she jerked them back, twisting them in her lap. Was he terminally ill? Was this some attempt to get his affairs in order? Her eyes skittered between him and the visiting teenagers fresh from snowboarding and seated at tables drinking hot chocolate. She wished Genesis were here interacting with other teens, meeting boys her age instead of somewhere sulking. Grace urged them to finish their snacks and head upstairs to the workshop on conflict resolution. Kamilah's mind was moving as slowly as churning homemade ice-cream with a crank freezer. "How long you plan on being in the area?"

Zende's fingers reached across the table and laid his atop her trembling ones. "Until I can convince you to come to Boston with me." His eyes looked at her intently. "Please hear me out?"

"That's not happening." Kamilah snapped through clenched teeth. These were the words she'd longed for since he'd abandoned her. His timing, like God's, was never convenient. "Does Reese know you're here?" She removed her fingers and drummed her hands on the table.

"Reese told me where to find you." Zende placed his hand on top of her drumming fingers, silencing them, maintaining the connection.

His heat seared through her body, awakening feelings she'd struggled to squelch. "If you came to rehash ancient history, call the driver, tell him to turn around, come back and drop you off at the nearest airport." She dropped her voice, eyes darting around at the few stragglers who were more interested in oversized chocolate chip cookies than any program offered by The Cathedral's staff.

"I'm not leaving. I can't sing with a voice like this." Zende tried to play on her sympathies. "I'm staying until I convince you I never stopped loving you."

She smirked. "You'll sing again. Two Grammys plus a bunch of other nominations. Stellar Awards. Performances on BET." She didn't care about any of that. Every time she listened to his music, she'd spend listless days sorting through the smallest details of their relationship, asking herself again what she lacked. When Zende left for Brown, Kamilah was wrapped in a sexual haze and already planning for his return. She enrolled in the highly ranked Bermuda College. Over time, the emails and texts came less frequently. Zende returned to the island for Christmas break. Between hanging out with old friends and his parents' formal events, she rarely saw him. She saw him for two days when he came home at the end of his first semester.

For the next three years, he flew home for official family functions when his presence was required. While he alerted her to his comings and goings, his time was primarily dedicated to family. She didn't try to insert herself where she was not wanted. His parents and siblings were awkward when she encountered them on the island. His parents were relieved when Reese graduated from Senior School with honors, and the Thompkins siblings left Bermuda.

Intent on letting Reese pursue university without her by his side, Kamilah transferred to Savannah College of Art and Design in Savannah, Georgia to complete her undergraduate degree and pursue advanced studies. At the end of her first year at SCAD, Zende flew out to Savannah and spent the weekend wining, dining, and romancing her. On Sunday, he told her he was moving to Boston to make a name for himself. He said nothing about their future. She let him go and decided to move on with her life. She began dating, even took a lover. She couldn't commit to building a lasting relationship with the man.

Kamilah no longer followed Zende's career. She used to scour the entertainment papers for news of his performances, music videos, or collaborations with high profile actors in Los Angeles. When his wedding announcement made the trade papers, she'd gone into seclusion for a month where she rehashed every encounter to grasp what it was about Zende that kept her loving him. Her voice quivered, "Why didn't you come back for me or be honest enough to say you'd moved on?"

"You were grieving the damage to your dancing career. You were primed to become a great ballerina before the accident, and then your parents were lost at sea." Zende faced her. He refused to drop his eyes. "I love you and want you with me."

Kamilah raised an eyebrow and shook her head as if trying to erase the teenaged dancer who'd stood on her toes, pointed, and pirouetted before extending her left leg straight up into the air.

Seventeen had been her year of challenge, but Kamilah met each test with an inborn steel spine. Kamilah was a member of the teenage dance troupe performing traditional island dances for cruise passengers who'd come ashore from ships docked in St. George. The younger dancer behind Kamilah lost her footing and crashed into Kamilah with enough force to topple her over the edge of the stage. With nothing to grab onto Kamilah fell four feet, crumpling to the concrete floor in front of the astounded audience. The leg was set by an inexperienced orthopedic surgeon who was not capable of dealing with the extensive damage. When she healed, Kamilah walked with a pronounced limp. Already slightly overweight, her weight ballooned.

Zende closed his eyes, and when he opened them, she saw the regret. "Please...let me explain. After college graduation and some initial success in Los Angeles, my parents finally accepted I could make it in the unpredictable music industry. I was ready to commit to a lasting relationship with you. Figuring you'd be on the verge of letting Reese fly solo, I flew to Savannah, a ring in my pocket and a sales contract waiting to be signed on a condo."

"Nobody told me." Kamilah's eyes were desolate. She turned away, unwilling to listen to him.

He crossed his long legs at the ankle, absently rubbing his hands on his thighs. "Your former housemate informed me you were gonna be gone for at least six months. You and ya boo eloped to Europe while he promoted his latest CD. It was months later before I figured out you and Reese were stickin' it to people."

"Cutting Reese out of my life has never been an option." She cleared her throat, picked up the red candle and dazzling wreath in the center of the table. "We were in Serbia."

"Doing what?"

"Reese had the top surgery … a total mastectomy with a resection of the breast and recontouring the chest for a more masculine appearance and a total hysterectomy. Europe has some of the best-trained transition surgeons in the world, and the people are more civilized about sexual identity and gender reassignment." She clarified matter-of-factly, wrapping, and placing the candle in the green plastic tub next to her chair.

"Whatcha mean?" His shocked voice rose. Reese was no longer "posing." Like most people, Zende had no real idea about "the change process," only the tidbits of gossip from LA cocktail parties and the tattletale rags about the personal lives of Hollywood stars.

Tears spurted from her eyes. Kamilah turned to look out the window facing the out-of-doors until her composure returned. "Reese was humiliated by what happened in St. George's. After you went to Brown, he started testosterone therapy, weightlifting, and running. By the time my brother graduated, he had facial hair, a deep voice and an Adam's apple. He was too young for the operation. Besides, we didn't have the money. He completed the legal name change before we left Bermuda. His end game was to earn enough money to pay for the sexual reassignment surgery."

"Women have to be falling all over his physique and firm jawline. Some of them would kick you to the curb so fast you'd have skid marks on your butt." Zende paused and continued soberly. "Milah, you're dying so Reese can continue to live a life wrapped in fairy dust. He created this fantasy, and it's not going to end well. There's no stage director to say 'cut' or to write an ending killing off the bad guys while he flies off to the stratosphere."

She laughed at the truth embedded in his statement. She could write books about young and old women pushing up on Reese. Milah shifted her glasses to the top of her head and pinched the bridge of her nose. "You don't know what it's like to live in fear of exposure. Men, women and now this little girl in the church are nothing if not persistent. This teenager could teach lessons to some of the grown women who cry on my shoulder."

"Why are women telling you their personal bizness?"

"It comes with the territory. 'First Lady' is supposed to be a listening ear, a leaning post for women in the church. I learned early on not to put Reese in situations that give the appearance of impropriety. Not everybody comes to church seeking salvation. Some women are looking for a man who might already be someone else's husband. If not looking for a husband, it might be a boo or a sugar daddy. We've heard all the lies and deception ... my son needs a man around... I need counseling."

Zende raised an eyebrow, shaking his head at her recitation and checked out the women in the atrium going about their chores.

"We instituted active youth programs throughout the week with a variety of positive male and female role models to spread the caregiving around. Someone can always ferret out the potential traps. Plus, it's insurance for any minister here who gets accused of inappropriate sexual contact. We're able to explain to law enforcement, families, and the busybodies how we attempt to protect kids and young adults around here. We have a back-up system to help kids and adults."

"Reese is lucky to have numerous associates."

"Prayer calls are handled by the associate pastors unless there's a specific reason for Reese to be involved. One-on-one counseling is done at the church. Grace sits in if it's a single woman. One of Reese's friends lost his preaching credentials last year. He had an affair with a woman who sought him out for marital counseling. She also wanted a little something sexual on the side. After she seduced the pastor, she blackmailed him into continuing the affair. When he broke it off, she went to the church leaders with video and taped phone calls."

"I never knew the job was more than standing up and delivering a message on Sunday morning."

"In a megachurch, the senior pastor is like the CEO of a multimillion-dollar corporation. He must have Superman's x-ray vision and Professor Charles Xavier of X-Men's ability to read minds. ... There's a woman who's trying to destroy Reese and the church." Her mask slid back in place.

"Talk to me. Maybe I can help you figure it out." Zende lived in the fast lane. He'd witnessed men and women conned by masters of the game. He'd learned about disastrous gang rape episodes and people rebuffed because of fetishes. When an iPhone was now a recording device, privacy was out the window.

"I'm not sure I can trust you. You drop in here, in the middle of a snowstorm."

"The truth is no matter what I did, who I was with, you weren't there. Providence and polyps dictated I come here. Being stranded in Chicago was God's sign to stop being a jackass and man up. Can't you tell me what's happening? The way I look at it, Reese owes his life to me."

"So now you're blackmailing me?" Milah laughed a shaky sound. "Let me think about it." She sucked in a deep breath, brushed her hair back with her hand. "Don't push ... and keep your hands off me! I'm not the same girl I was at seventeen."

Zende flinched, "Milah, do you love me?"

Kamilah put her hands over her cheeks and brushed back tears. "Love is not the issue. You can't say you adore me, seduce me, leave me, and not come back. You can't come in here as if the years apart didn't happen and ask anything of me. Damn you, Zende. You were one hundred miles from Bermuda, yet you had no time to come to check on me. Then you went to LA and asked another woman to marry you."

"I'm here now to make it work."

"Your family won't accept Reese in any form. We," she pushed her hands together, "me and Reese, we're all we got."

How many times had she reminded Zende of that fact? "You need to slow this train down."

"Let me stay until you believe I've changed."

CHAPTER NINE:
ZENDE

LATE THAT EVENING, Zende watched the silent communication passing between brother and sister. Truly little had changed. The siblings were in sync—a bond forged as children, tested and still resilient. While eating tasty foods that reminded him of home: planked salmon; plantains; mixed vegetables; and sour cream pound cake, the three old friends bantered back and forth about their Bermuda mischief-making, music and finally about how the Thompkins survived in this small community. Zende was still missing a link about why they were masquerading as a couple instead of acknowledging their familial ties.

Zende studied Kamilah's transformation. Not only was she beautiful with her stylish outfit of moss green slacks, brightly patterned angora sweater, and soft-soled shoes, but she'd gained the poise and sophistication she lacked as a teenager. Her thick hair inherited from her mother, Saraya, was unbound, flowing down her back. Flawless make-up and jewelry bespoke her position as First Lady. Kamilah's natural beauty was enhanced by the twenty-five pounds she'd lost since the last time he'd seen her.

Kamilah prepared a pot of Bermuda Coffee LTD's illy brand coffee and then excused herself, claiming she had a raging headache. The two men moved to Reese's home office to drink the fragrant coffee. "Zende, you wantta stay here indefinitely in one of the condos and tell me you are stealing Milah?" Reese steepled his hands as he considered Zende's request to stay while he worked on some new music ideas and convinced Kamilah to leave him. "This doesn't feel right to me."

"I won't put her in a compromising position." Zende twisted his tight shoulders and settled into a comfortable position. "Man, this sex change shit is too deep for me. Other than gossip and men's locker room humor, sexual identity is not a topic I can have an honest conversation about."

Reese cast a rueful glance at him. "No one does. Try living it. Being called a 'two-hole freak'. Watching as the fat migrates from your hips and butt to your gut after testosterone injections. Trying to shop in the men's department with nosy salesclerks forgetting to knock on closed doors." Reese sat back with his arms folded across his chest. His body was toned and muscular beneath the sweater and leather slacks.

Zende couldn't fathom how the physical transformation occurred. His visual was of the skinny thirteen-year-old girl with short curly hair, dressed like a boy who would fight or cut anyone who dared to call her a girl or a derogatory name. "Your male bonding was slim to none back in the day."

Reese snorted and stared at him. "You were one of my principal tormentors back then."

Zende felt guilty for his pettiness. "Okay, I was an asshole." Zende wanted Reese gone. The girl who believed she was a boy made him uncomfortable. Zende tried to accept Reese because Milah loved him. But the idea of a *girly* boy freaked him out. As a result, Zende was rude and insensitive to the younger child's struggle. Had it not been for their shared love of music and the theatre, Zende would have been as cruel to Reese as the other kids. He also knew Milah and Reese were a team, and he would be the loser if he forced her to choose.

"I've come a long way," Reese acknowledged. "There are some Chicago musicians I jam with when I'm in the city. I befriended some regular guys who became dudes to drink with, shoot pool and bowl with. If you hang around longer than two days, I'll challenge you to a game of pool."

63

Zende snickered, unable to imagine Reese shooting pool and drinking beer with a bunch of loud-mouthed working stiffs. The man in front of Zende carried himself with assurance and elegance. "You not getting rid of me until we resolve this situation." The past couldn't be changed, but a future without Kamilah by his side was too high a price to pay for stubbornness and pride.

Reese picked up a ball of rubber bands on the table next to his chair, negligently throwing it up and down, squeezing it as if strangling someone, then throwing it up again. Reese leaned back in his reclining chair until the stand kicked out and he crossed one leg over the other. "It hasn't been one big do-over. When I was going back and forth to Chicago for therapy, I met a woman. We started kicking it." Reese's eyes softened before the icy façade jolted back in. A bitter smile hovered around the man's mouth. "Flirty skirts n sheer tops showing off ample breasts, small waist and flared hips. We'd go dancing, laugh, and drink shots." Reese reached for the crystal glass, sipping more rum and watching the action on the television screen. "Taking it as slow as molasses dripping from the holes bored in trees during winter."

"Before the top surgery?" Zende asked, glad Kamilah had clued him in on the terminology for a total mastectomy and hysterectomy.

"Yep." Reese popped up from the chair, ambled over to the étagère and pointed to three Grammys.

Zende was fascinated by Reese's music and the recognition the artist received during his European tour. The haunting lyrics and blue/black/purple notes underlying some of Reese's most celebrated music reminded him of Bonnie Raitt's work. The last few pieces of the puzzle of Reese Thompkins' transition slid into place. The quality of work Reese recorded had the distinctive characteristics of a person in love and using music to take gigantic leaps into the future.

Reese strolled down memory lane. "I passed the pre-surgery time refining my sound, going into the studio, and laying down tracks. On the weekends I did some musical arrangements with a variety of acts, especially drummers, strings and percussionists at some of Chicago's best jazz spots." The smile was genuine, the pride evident as Reese looked back on a period of growth and acceptance.

Zende asked the essential question. "Did her knowing what's up make the physical relationship less awkward?"

Reese frowned as though letting go of the dream. "She acted like she was cool with it ... but she wasn't." His posture resembled snow draped over an ice sculpture left outside in this weather. Reese set the crystal down as though afraid of snapping the expensive glass. "She never invited me to meet her family or friends. It was only later when the pieces rearranged themselves into a different image that I questioned what the hell happened to me."

"Did you confront her? Say hey, what's with the secrecy?" Zende inquired.

Reese pounded his forehead with his fist. "Our dates were to bars in Boys Town, the movies, her apartment or my hotel room." His voice dropped. He bit his lower lip. "We were hot and heavy for nine months. Without warning, she broke it off."

"That must have been a kick in the nuts—metaphorically?" Zende walked over to his old adversary and laid his hand on Reese's stooped shoulder. Reese was solid muscle. Zende needed to pay attention to the physical changes in Reese instead of the picture he carried of a young teen struggling to be treated like a man.

Reese's dammed up hurt and humiliation burst like a stream overflowing its boundaries at the end of the winter. "Six months later, she married a dude she'd known since grammar school. The marriage lasted less than a year."

Desperation clawed at Zende. He was in way over his head. When he came here, he was solely focused on extricating Kamilah from Reese, not wading into deep unchartered waters. "Does she know you had the top surgery?"

Reese's mouth tightened. His eyes flashed. "She was the first person I called when the bandages came off. She asked why I hadn't done the top and bottom surgeries at the same time. I hung up on her."

Zende empathized with the pain and despair in Reese's clenched facial features, stiff neck, and haunted eyes. The woman emasculated him and still had her hooks in his gut.

"Man, no offense, but I want to know the same thing. Why not do it all at once and get it over with? Move on." Reese's story was more complicated than Zende bargained for. Since Reese was either going to be a liability or an asset in his campaign to liberate Kamilah, Zende had to rethink his relationship with the person who would be his brother-in-law. "Explain to me why you didn't finish the job."

Reese jutted out his chin. "Three reasons. Uncertainty. Pain. Money." Reese held up three fingers. He sounded weary as if tired of explaining to stupid people. "Reassignment surgery is long and painful. It's not one surgery. It's multiple small surgeries, skin grafts, and healing time. The recovery takes months. You remember how skinny I was. I had to do bodybuilding and body sculpting." Reese's mouth opened and closed. All the suppressed humiliation, trauma, rejections, popped like the cork on fine wine. "When the doctors scheduled the surgery, Milah gave up her life in Savannah to accompany me to Europe."

And ruined Zende's plans. "She's sacrificed her life for your self-gratification."

"Most people in my situation are disowned, disinherited and thrown out like yesterday's garbage." Reese's eyes pleaded with Zende. "You better be serious this time. You broke her heart." Reese blew out a long, slow breath.

Snapping between concern and self-interest, Zende barked at Reese. "Your life is built on a lie. The longer it goes on, the more chances of harm to Kamilah. She deserves her own family, children, and career. Stop being so damn self-centered. Think about Milah. Not the self-sacrificing big sister who loves you, but the beautiful stifled woman when there's no excuse for it."

Reese squeezed the bands, the tendons in his hands standing out. "Zende, I'm not as self-absorbed as you think. The woman... my former lover put a target on my back. She wants to destroy everything I've worked to build. I have a plan. It's got some loose ends that need to be tied up. I need a little more time to fix this mess."

"And while you're working on this grand scheme, find a woman who's into you. Be honest with her."

Reese loosened his fingers from around the band, dropping it on the table, flexed his fingers. "I haven't ruled out having a family someday."

Zende spoke from his heart. "I'm serving notice on you. I intend to snatch Milah away from here. She deserves more even if you're determined to exist in this half-life."

Reese was silent for several minutes.

When Zende couldn't take the silence any longer, he interjected, "Man, I'm beggin' you to see how selfish you're being. You'll always be her baby brother. Don't make me fight you for her. All three of us will lose."

Reese's stiff shoulders dropped, and he rubbed his hands across his face. "Damn man, when did you grow up? Stop being so shallow?"

"When it came time to marry a woman I didn't love."

Reese nodded as if coming to a decision. "We'll put out your story about your health, the sabbatical and the weather. We'll acknowledge the family connection and tell people you're gonna be hanging around and living in one of the condos. Skeptics can check you out on social media for verification. Act like you working. Keep a schedule in the studio."

"And you'll give us some time to reconnect without scowling every minute."

"I'll give you some privacy. Milah can determine if she wants to be with you." Reese laid down the rules. "You can't stay at our place past midnight. You're a guest at The Cathedral. A visitor wouldn't monopolize his host by being underfoot all the damn time."

CHAPTER TEN:
REESE

THE FOLLOWING MORNING REESE'S hawkish gaze looked around the almost full sanctuary. The bitterly cold weather never kept the faithful at home. Reese's gaze slid onto young families with playful children who were unable to sit still. Some overprotective mothers were reluctant to send toddlers to the nursery program equipped with trained and qualified staff. His eyes searched the teenagers congregated in the upper balcony. There'd been no sign of Genesis this morning. No Misty either. He sent up a quick prayer for mother and daughter.

The organist's final riff of the opening prelude brought him out of his reverie. Reese joked with the congregation. "The storm blew in an old friend. He got stranded in Chicago on the way to Boston which got hit worse than us with twenty-four inches of snow."

The congregation groaned, glad they were only getting two or three inches of snow each day. It was still piling up enough to make driving conditions hazardous and to keep numerous people stranded in their homes.

Reese's brown eyes settled on a squirming Zende. "Due to some health challenges and a little throat surgery, he can't sing right now. But he can lay down some tracks with me." He winked at Zende and shrugged his shoulders. "We're setting him up in the studio to record some real music and to make him earn his keep. Maybe we'll set up a collaboration or two with the Gospel Choir since we gotta feed and house him for a while."

The congregation's eyes followed Reese's gaze to the man sitting next to First Lady Kamilah. Zende waggled his fingers at him, pointing an imaginary gun and pulling the trigger. Enthusiastic clapping, catcalls, and whistling erupted around the sanctuary.

"And we can embarrass family. His voice may be resting, but his hands aren't." Reese extended his long slim fingers to the second row. "Zende Lightbourn!! Church, treat him like family."

The congregation exploded at the mention of his name. Zende's star had rocketed toward the stratosphere since pursuing a career in music. His dreads flew as his muscular body pounded out music on the keyboard or drums. He was a featured artist on awards shows and telethons promoting international causes such as the 2004 Indonesian tsunami, the 2010 earthquake in Haiti and childhood hunger.

Whistles.

"Zende!"

"Come on up here and give us a musical selection … or two."

Flamboyant in black dress slacks and a purple suede jacket with silver studs, Zende strode confidently to Steve Bartholomew, the mixed-gray-haired brother on the keyboard, who moved over to make room for him. After speaking to Steve, the keyboardist left his seat to talk with the four other musicians. Zende's long fingers caressed the Yamaha professional keyboard as if the instrument were the woman he loved. The drummer, acoustic guitar player, bass player, and trumpeter joined in. The congregation hummed and swayed in tempo with the music… *How Great Thou Art.* The melody seeped into the congregants' souls, touching wounded places, and causing spirits to soar.

Judson Stubblefield, the lanky choir director, stood, raised his hands and the two-hundred-fifty-member choir rose as one. With his outstretched hand, the long-limbed man looked at Zende, back at the choir and the trained singers opened their mouths, and synchronized music poured out. *How ... Great ... Thou ... Art!* The congregation raised their hands. Clapping. Crying. Members stood to their feet. The spirit of God preserved in traditional music moved them higher than their ordinary circumstances.

Reese pulled out his handkerchief and mopped his face as Zende's artistry visibly moved his congregation. Zende's teeth were biting his lower lip, straining not to sing as his skilled hands wrung emotions from his soul and poured them into the song.

"Amen. Amen. Brother Lightbourn." Voices erupted all over the sanctuary.

Reese, stirred by Zende's overwhelming music, opened his mouth, and sang, "... my soul ... my Savior God to Thee ...How Great Thou Art!" The celebration of life in the music transported him back to when they were Bermuda's two best young musicians and fiercest competitors. The sanctuary exploded with the combination of shouts, hand clapping, and foot stomping. Zende transitioned into several of his original pieces, showing off the range of his musical abilities to an enthusiastic audience who were experiencing an impromptu concert with an international singer/musician.

At the close of service, parishioners surrounded Zende. They asked him to sign bulletins and other decorative scraps of paper. The boldest ones put documents containing their phone numbers in his hand. Reese's shoulders moved in mirth, having been the recipient of similar behavior.

CHAPTER ELEVEN:
REESE

"Morning, Grace. What's got you up this early?" Grace Winston was already ensconced in her usual seat, leafing through a counseling manual, waiting for the Monday morning ministerial staff meeting. Seven men and women with divinity degrees and varying years in ministry aided Reese in operating the various departments. The clergy ranged in age from mid-twenties to the early sixties and serviced the thousands of people on the rolls as well as new converts and the endless number of services and tasks necessary to operate on a grand scale. He was freed up to concentrate on church leadership and musical pursuits.

The happenings of the past week hindered the senior pastor's worship and praise, leaving him anxious and uncertain. He picked up the remote control and let the Gospel Choir's latest CD pour into the room. The up-tempo music soothed his nerves and restored his sanity.

The cafeteria staff had set out a warming tray filled with hot breakfast sandwiches, fresh fruit, yogurt, coffee, hot water, and juice. Reese poured coffee into a stainless-steel mug and lifted the pot in Grace's direction.

Grace dipped her head affirmatively. "Three packets of artificial sweetener and a lot of cream." Grace considered herself mentoring Reese whether he wanted her in his business or not. She also subtly reminded him she was privy to gossip and innuendo from people who didn't support the pastor. "You're questioning why I encroach on your time when you need to be reflecting on whose making demands, disrupting your agenda and what the payback is gonna be."

Loading up the coffee, he chuckled and handed it to her. "A little coffee with your cream and sugar, ma'am." His meditation time made a break for the window.

"Yep!" Reese was accustomed to listening, sifting, taking what was useful and ignoring the rest of her chatter. He came right to the point. "Grace, what happened with Genesis on Friday can't happen again. We're going to have to set some stricter guidelines for the youth ministry. I don't want to limit the opportunities for the teenagers to be in the Winston House but sneaking into our private space is not acceptable."

"You can't blame all of the kids for Genesis' antics? She's been trying to get your attention for months! Whatever is going on with her is beyond the church's ability to handle. There are rumors she's hosting after school parties. Some guy who flunked out of college lives in the unit below her and Misty. He's supplying the liquor and weed. Some of the parents no longer let their daughters hang out with her."

"How long has this been going on? What is the point of these weekly meetings if staff withholds critical information from me?"

"Since last fall. His buddies went back to college, so he befriended Genesis. Misty is gone a lot in the evenings, and as long as the kids are gone before Misty gets home, everybody's cool." Grace sounded concerned like she had finally gotten a clue that one of her charges was in deeper trouble than even she'd recognized. "My source says it's gotten out of control. A girl, not one of the kids who come here with Genesis, got high and several boys had sex with her."

"How did you get the 4-1-1?" Reese stared at Grace. None of them had a clue about the extent of Genesis' acting out behavior. The potential for harm to herself or someone else was endless.

"When Genesis didn't come back to the youth retreat on Saturday, I sat down with some of her close buds for a chat.

They told the story. The girl who was sexually assaulted woke up bleeding and sore. Then she saw the condoms. When she threatened Genesis, the parties stopped for a while. Our girl's back at it with a different crew." Grace tapped on her cup with her pen, frustration in every tap. "Genesis has been bragging about getting it on with the college dropout."

"Did you contact Misty?"

"I went over there Saturday evening after the group session ended. Misty didn't believe any of it. Genesis lied and said the girl was a slut. Misty said nothing was going on, but she told Genesis not to have any more kids over when she wasn't home. Mother and daughter live in different time zones. You didn't see her on Friday night."

"I heard about it."

"Not the same. That girl is either going to self-destruct or she's going to make her mother hurt her. She needs punishment, consequences, and counseling."

"Then, alert whoever on the Ministry team has a need to know. Let's get a plan together with some teeth in it. I've got too much going on to worry about sexual harassment from a sixteen-year-old or a sex scandal involving young people in our programs."

"Leave it to me." Grace winked at him and spoke in conspiratorial tones. "I hear the deacons are taking a bite out of your hind parts over the project."

"What are you hearing?" Why did he ask stupid questions when he already knew? Grace was settling for an affair with a married man instead of making a life for herself without the crutch of this place.

She pointed one manicured finger toward him, "You and I don't lie to each other, Pastor Reese. You've seen Marcelle leaving my house before daylight on numerous occasions."

"You deserve better than him. It's hard not to punch his sanctimonious face sometimes."

Grace tossed her head, smirking. Her voice softened. "Here's a tidbit of information that might help you understand his point of view."

"Please inform me." Reese stuffed strawberries in his mouth, but not because he was hungry. They kept him from saying what he really felt about Marcelle cheating on his wife with his youth director.

"Deacon Grimm's going to ruin this project because if it goes forward, he'll be publicly embarrassed." Grace delivered the killing blow. "He can't contribute any money to the campaign."

Reese choked on the berries. He grabbed a napkin and spit out the food to clear his throat. "And.... that's a reason to stop this project?" Why would a grown man throw a temper tantrum when the truth would be more straightforward? "Couldn't he have said I gotta sit this one out?"

Here came the voice he hated. Explaining. Telling. "He's been let go from his job as Chief Financial Officer for Peoria County. The County Board gave him a severance package which lets him act big for another six months or so if he's careful."

The praise music pouring out of the surround sound gave Reese pause. He slowed his heart rate. "We have to act before we get cited for not taking down the current Tower."

"Marcelle's always the primary giver. He gave the first twenty percent for Pastor Winston's memorial."

"And we know why?" Big Poppa needing to look prosperous in the eyes of his mistress. "His bullshit is overriding the needs of the church." Reese tapped his hands and feet along with the drum section of the CD. "So, he can poke out his barrel chest and remind the congregation he's Deacon Grimm, planning to be the head deacon when Deacon Slay steps aside." He adopted his father's pet saying: one monkey don't stop any show. "The project can proceed without him."

Grace jerked out of her comfortable position, sitting up ramrod straight. "You're smart, Pastor Reese." She drank her coffee, then spoke calmly, carefully. "Your honeymoon here has been over for a while. You getting ready to see the real politics of The Cathedral when you ask the membership to step up and stop playing church, quit talking 'bout how much they love the Lord and pay money over and above what they want to give."

He pushed his chair closer to Grace, taking her measure and reminding her, "The Broadcast Tower is key to our ability to broadcast the Word outside the confines of the building, to bring in the donations to keep us vibrant and growing. If your 'friend' can look beyond his ego, he'll see this was never about him, his ego, or upstaging him."

CHAPTER TWELVE:
REESE

REESE CONVENED A SMALL committee of trusted individuals he'd worked with over the past five years: Head Deacon Slay; Assistant Pastor Everett Thornton; Tanji Mitchell, Communication's Director, and his Director of Administration, Rennett Ford. Reese knew their aptitudes and work ethic. If they caught the vision, they'd take his fundraising outline and revise it to accomplish the goal. He provided them with the scope of work to raise five million dollars. He shared scripts, spreadsheets, targets, and goals they would be expected to reach. Reese finished by saying, "Everett, I need you to walk alongside me and be the point person for the congregation to talk to. Grimm has decided I'm the enemy for asking the church members to rebuild the Tower.

The assistant pastor shook his head, clearly confused. "The storm happened in November, and two months later we still don't have a plan. Have the deacons read the reports from the inspectors and the insurance company? The current tower was built before they enacted new codes for such structures. The city is going to condemn the tower if the church doesn't take action soon."

Reese shook his head at the small-minded men who couldn't differentiate between personal agendas and "real" business. "Grimm's making it a contest to ask the church to choose his leadership over mine. He knows Deacon Slay is on dialysis and will have to step down if he doesn't get a kidney transplant. He expects to be named head deacon."

Rennett had a master's degree in organizational development. Her skills complimented Reese's management style, and she always kept his office on point. "Does he have an alternative plan?"

Deacon Slay shared what was said at the deacons' meeting. "Throw up something that can be covered by insurance. It won't have the same range as we have now because the technology standards have changed. The Cathedral will have less communication capacity than we have now. Our insurance will have to be updated or changed after they pay off this claim."

The assistant minister chuckled. "He's trying to kick the can down the road. This is not the Congress of the United States. We have to pay our bills as they come due."

"What's his second option?" The Director of Administration queried the group.

"That I finance the rebuilding with profits from the production studio's surpluses." Reese sneered. "Winston overbuilt the property without bringing in new members or new revenue sources. His mantra was God will provide."

The assistant pastor raised his eyes to heaven, drummed his fingers on the table and shook his head.

Reese added dramatically. "That's why I need you to be involved. The congregation can't view this as 'what the pastor wants'. It's about how we reach more people and, yes, bring in revenue to keep The Cathedral growing and thriving."

The assistant pastor shook his head in disgust. "We won't depend on the production studio to finance the church." His voice rose. "When are you going to turn in your resignation? You postponed it for the clean-up, and now there's another issue. Pastor Reese, let the deacons figure it out on their own."

Reese shook his head. "This is between you, me and God. God is going to get the glory, not Grimm, for rebuilding the Tower."

***

Late in the morning, Deacons Hudson, Grimm and White, the unholy trio of chaos and confusion, ambushed Reese in his office while he was preparing Sunday's message. They knew this was his alone time to petition God for the words and examples to reveal discernment, provide spiritual nourishment or lift some burdens from his congregation. Lately, he was the supplicant asking God to open his eyes.

"Pastor, we called for the deacons to review your contract and buy you out. You are on notice." Deacon Hudson didn't even bother with the usual pleasantries. Deacon Grimm had primed Deacon Hudson to be the spokesman with bold words, but the body and voice were frail.

"Do you want to replace me today?" Reese stood up but made no move to walk over and shake their hands. He didn't want their intrusion, but he had to remain gracious. He was an adult. He motioned for them to sit at a table. They ought to read their documents. Only the Head Deacon had the authority to fire the pastor or ask for his resignation. If anyone could fire the pastor on a whim, there was no need for an employment contract drafted by a lawyer, signed and witnessed.

Deacon Grimm sat his bulk in a chair and led with his weak trump card. "Members been callin' us. They don't want any parts of this mess. You smiled, confused them, and manipulated them into this fiasco. Made 'em feel like they wanted this plan of yours. The members don't." Grimm knew about building codes, violations, and fines. Had Reese come to him first, Grimm would have taken credit for saving the church. He needed to be the savior. His stature was being undermined by this inexperienced preacher.

White crossed his arms. As usual, he tried to appease both sides. "The bad weather causing people to miss work, Pastor. Gon' be a couple of short work weeks, maybe months."

Reese's eyebrows went up. How did the two shysters pull White into this disaster? Probably disguised it as concern for the membership's finances. The corners of Reese's mouth turned up. He figured Grimm had only given his surrogates one-liners but didn't provide anything for the follow-up confrontation. He nodded. "If the weather forecasters are right, it's either going to be a short month or a long winter."

"Not funny." Grimm's righteous indignation was one of his best bullying tactics. His threatening bulk was marred by Reese unsuccessfully hiding a smirk when envisioning his lard ass in a pair of women's silk panties. Grace let that juicy tidbit slip. The visual added a new insult to the phrase "put your big girl panties on."

"We know the part-time workers are having trouble making ends meet." The servant leader mused, "What're you hearing from the majority of members who work salaried jobs?"

The two older men's faces fell. They looked to Grimm for support.

"Deacon Grimm, we never counted on one-hundred-percent support." Reese almost felt sorry for the man who saw control slipping away from him. He'd always been the shot-caller and big baller at The Cathedral.

Grimm grumbled, "Money grubbing bastard..."

Reese wanted to throw his African paperweight at them. The deacons' job was to support the church, not use their position to settle scores or aggrandize themselves. The Cathedral provided extensive outreach and financial services to members in their time of need. He reminded them of the "money-grubbing" going on around here. "The church makes mortgage payments to keep folks from being foreclosed on. We buy food. We've paid college tuition when financial aid didn't come through. We pay funeral costs for members' wayward children who die unexpectedly without any life insurance. The church picks up the balance of the costs to the funeral home for seniors who bought those cheap burial policies fifty years ago and don't have ten thousand dollars' worth of insurance at the time of their death. And you call me money-grubbing."

These assholes were not going to ruin his day, interrupt this time with God, then walk away unscathed. "Rennett," Reese spoke into the console to his assistant, "bring the call logs and print out the accounting sheets of the money we've received so far. Then, call Rev. Thornton and cancel our meeting while I share our progress with the deacons. Please have someone bring lunch over to me."

Reese turned his attention back to three bewildered faces. The deacons knew better than to come ill-prepared to reinterpret the two or three phone calls they received rather than ask for the facts. "If you need me to pull up the video of Wednesday's message, I can." He picked up the remote device, pointed it at the wall screen, and hit Enter. He scrolled down to the passage in question and pushed Play with the sound on. "I asked the members to settle this matter in their hearts and give accordingly. No assessments. No keeping track of who does not give." Reese turned up the volume and watched as White and Hudson shuffled their feet, shrinking in their clothes. He turned off the sound and let the video continue.

Although the man outweighed him by almost two hundred pounds, Reese reserved his sharpest criticism for Marcelle Grimm. Reese said, "I don't know who you talkin to, Deacon, but I'll bet you my next month's salary the people who say no will be the first ones to call for the pastor and the church in times of distress; we never say *no*." Active pastoring wore a man down and sometimes made him doubt God as the architect of the modern church. Legalism often replaced relationships with God. Petty egos found an outlet in dictating to God's anointed how to operate the church.

Grimm's nose flared. He cursed under his breath as his finger stalled over a name on the list. "There's so-and-so Benin. He musta had a change of heart." Hudson and White shot him quizzical looks. Grimm stared at the muted screen and pounded his fist on the table.

"You told us Benin said *until God himself shows me a sign, I'm not giving a damn dime.*"

God must have given Brother Benin a giant blinking sign by the number of zeros on the gift. The three elders perused the statements. The names and amounts didn't square up with their "lack of support for the project" or for rethinking Pastor Reese's contract. Since Wednesday night, over $100,000 had been paid by church members. The office staff received emails indicating more funds would come in as soon as members received their paychecks.

"Humph!" Grimm uttered, "I'm through." Grimm picked up the sheaf of papers and pointed his beefy fist at Reese. His fellow deacons looked dumbfounded.

This latest reenactment of the War Between The States was not going to end unless one of them backed down or left.

Reese had won this battle, but the civil war raged on. The imp in him asked, "With me, the church, or God?" Leaning forward and drumming his fingers on the desk, Reese quipped, "Feels like you're playing gotcha, gentlemen. It's been less than a week since we started the fundraising and you already calling the project a failure. Most people are still making up their minds one way or the other. I acquiesced on the thirty-day timeline and agreed to let the people decide." Reese let the tension build until their squirming signaled an end of the fake bravado. He was spending three to four hours a day speaking to local philanthropists and businesses sharing the importance of new construction versus a patch job. Each one asked for a proposal, saying they would respond as quickly as their organizations could review the request.

Reese rubbed his face and pointed at Deacon Hudson. "This project is neither a pissing contest nor whose-in-charge moment. Since you're the leader of this delegation, explain to me exactly how you, Deacon Grimm and Deacon White are gonna replace the Tower. Is it your strategy to let it short out and burn up every circuit board, computer, and appliance in The Cathedral?"

The men examined the papers in front of them, unable to meet his gaze.

"Let me remind you of the information in the report shared at the meeting where you didn't want to take up the proposed plan."

"We don't wantta hear it." Grimm, the bully, had been outmaneuvered by the class nerd.

"This is not a game, gentlemen." Pastor Reese pointed to copies of his original presentation still stacked up on the table. "One. The Cathedral was cited for having an unsafe structure on its property. If the current structure topples, it's going to cause a lot of damage to the church and to anyone who happens to be in the vicinity. What the insurance company will pay out won't cover the cost of new construction."

Grimm grumbled under his breath. "Bullshit scare tactics."

Ignoring Grimm, Reese continued reading from the report. "Two. If a lightning strike hits the partially grounded wires and starts a fire, our commercial insurance won't cover the damage. The tower has to come down."

"We ain't rich." Hudson said *no* although evidence to the contrary meant there was a financial cost. At eighty, he'd seen preachers make outrageous promises. He didn't believe this young preacher could deliver on this undertaking.

"We're going to have to raise the money from somewhere to rebuild." Reese pressed on. "We need to broadcast our message to reach more souls. There's a lot of folks tuned into Bedside-Baptist-Methodist-Pentecostal-Nondenominational television on Sunday morning. Maybe we can convince them to come and join us." The inclement weather saved them from civil infractions. "You ought to be on your knees thanking God for this horrendous fall and winter."

"Why do you always have to hijack the conversation and take the decision out of our hands?" Finally. Deacon Hudson spoke his truth.

"Cause you want to get into a pissin' contest over E-V-E-R-Y-T-H-I-N-G." Reese fixed each man with a glare. "You are worse than teen boys fighting over who got the biggest dick?

Who cares?" Reese was disgusted with grown men whining and crying when they signed on to be the spiritual and moral leaders of the church.

There was a timid knock on the door. Reese was thankful for the interruption. His voice dropped to its standard register. "Come in."

Rennett entered and placed the covered tray on the pastor's desk. Reese lifted the lid, the mouth-watering smells wafting around the room. "Thanks, Rennett."

She turned and walked out of the room, closing the door softly behind her.

"You're on notice. We won't tolerate you acting as if you the last word around here." Grimm's face was a thundercloud.

Reese chortled. "God always has the last word, deacons. Come by the church tomorrow. In the vestibule, communications and fundraising staff will have set up the fundraising display, including a large thermometer to track giving from individuals and groups. The red temperature gauge will move up until we reach five million dollars. Pictures of individuals or organizations making contributions of fifty thousand dollars or more will also be displayed." Reese sat down, uncovered his food, and prayed. When he looked up, they were gone.

CHAPTER THIRTEEN: ZENDE

ZENDE FINALLY CONNECTED THE dots Noori had provided; he shoulda done so after reading the magazine article. Noori steered him in this direction because she had an ulterior motive to precipitate a confrontation between Reese and Zende. Instead of reacting like a recovering drunk knowing there was free beer in the next room, he didn't slow his roll long enough to ask why Noori Sherman remembered Kamilah from a photo sitting on his desk at Brown University. No way. Noori made a point to ask about Kamilah during dinner. She happened to have a copy of Kamilah's article in her condo. Instead, he'd demanded the concierge hire him a car and find a store where he could purchase jacket, boots, and winter clothing.

He went back over snippets of the conversations he and Kamilah had had since Saturday night.

"Reese has enemies."

"What progressive pastor doesn't? Nondenominational. Denominations. Church politics rule. Successful preachers build fences of righteousness around them, or they infiltrate the vipers' nest to discover what the opposition is planning to do." Zende responded to Kamilah's revelation while they were supposedly out sightseeing. He kept his eyes on the road as they drove around so he could get the lay of the community.

"Reese doesn't listen well to opinions not lining up with his vision." Kamilah saw the vultures swirling before Reese did. Small minded laymen who wanted to rule the church, enforce their brand of religiosity, and control God's Word.

"Same as he did at the theatre." Zende laughed, lifting his neck as if easing the tension from between his shoulders caused by the stilted conversation.

"Enemies crop up without him trying to offend." Milah ticked off the sins his critics placed on him. *"They say Reese's full of himself, arrogant, too well educated, has too much money, power, and prestige separate and apart from The Cathedral.*

"So why are you both still here?"

"After much prayer and soul-searching, Reese decided the end of last year was the time to move on. He'd addressed his resignation letter to Deacon Slay and planned to hand deliver it to him on the day the tornado struck. The only damage The Cathedral sustained was to the tower. A lot of our members and close neighbors were devastated. Four hundred houses were destroyed during twenty-seconds of Category Four winds. Then storms, looters and a small fire and police system ill-equipped to deal with a tornado caused the rest of the destruction. Reese is stubborn enough to believe God still has work for him to do here."

"Man, I owe you an apology." A contrite Zende entered Reese's production studio office, sat at the second keyboard in the corner and waited until Reese ended a vocal session with three young women. Reese was mentoring the group of college students who had excellent harmony but no unique fashion or movement style. The producer was pressing them to stop imitating other girl groups in favor of developing their own style. Eventually, the young women and the session engineer packed up and left the two men alone.

"Can they make it on the big stage?" Zende voiced his negative thoughts aloud. "A lot of hustlers out there will turn them into sexualized, drugged out ingénues. I've seen it too many times." While working side by side in the studio, Zende and Reese had achieved a sense of comfort with each other, if not comradery. As two powerfully skilled musicians, they complemented each other, added individualism and flair to whatever music they created together.

Reese shrugged. "We're gonna work with them. Teach 'em what we know about not hitching your reputation to mind-blowing sex and bad contracts that land you in bankruptcy court. After that, they have to want fame enough to work for it."

As Zende absentmindedly played the instrument, he explained calling Noori, having dinner with her. The princess of mean hadn't mentioned classmates they had in common although some were living in the Chicago metro area. But she made a point of sharing the magazine article about Kamilah. "Noori Sherman's conjuring up island mischief to wreck your relationship with Kamilah and the congregation. I'm reading between the lines of her conversation and what you told me about your mystery woman. My happening to come along gave her a convenient tool to use in this twisted game."

Reese gritted his teeth. It was a wonder his dentist kept him on as a patient. The man prescribed a mouth guard for nighttime wear, and Reese needed another one for daytime wear. He rocked on his feet as if organizing his thoughts. "If you hadn't come along, she'd have found another way to escalate the pressure." Reese prowled the space, his bunched fists punching at imaginary ghosts. "What's her endgame?"

"How did the two of you meet," Zende asked?

Reese sat, head down, hands between his legs, recalling, "Before surgery, I spent a year in weekly therapy sessions. My psychiatrist was affiliated with the university; she was Noori's boss. As part of the internship required to earn the Ph.D., Dr. Erickson assigned Noori to complete social histories on her new patients. Social histories are a prelude to an intensive evaluation of a patient's mental, physical, and emotional health.

We met for coffee a few times to fill out the forms and get the details straight." Reese raised hang dog eyes to Zende. "She started flirting with me on the second coffee date."

Zende riffed the chord he was working on, dispelling the surge of anger. He changed the notes to something mellower. "She was as wrong as old men wearing black socks and sandals on the Coco Reef Beach."

Reese snickered. "At least the old men were harmless. Noori's a boa constrictor."

Shaking his head, Zende's hands created a crashing sound on the keyboard. "You should have reported her."

Reese sat up, scraping his heels, and wrapping his hands around his chest, "I was tired of being treated like conjoined twins or the mustached lady in the circus." He paused. "I felt accepted and desired by an older woman."

"I'm not trying to bust your hallowed memories," Zende snorted. "But the Noori I remember from Brown was nice/nasty. She was smart but no one you wanted to cross." Zende walked over to the fridge and grabbed a bottle of Bermudan shandy, a type of beer mixed with lemonade. He opened it and drank deeply. "There was a story going around campus her freshman year. I didn't put much stock in it at the time."

"What was it?"

"That Noori lost her virginity to the captain of the football team. Dude laughed about it the next day. 'Black girl giving it up' was another notch on his bedpost."

"I bet she didn't take that well."

"Nope. The girl I was dating lived on the same floor, a few doors down from Noori. She says Noori was embarrassed as hell at lunch when other students were laughing and pointing at her. Her face was blotchy, eyes red and swollen. She looked like she hadn't had any sleep. However, Noori got back at the football player. She went to the next home game, sat with a group of loudmouths, told them despite the captain's bravado, he wasn't hung. His little dick was so barely there it wasn't worthy of her fine ass. So, technically, she was still a virgin."

"God, she killed him. Demeaning people seems to be her stock in trade." Reese remembered his shame of being unmasked, scared of escalating violence or death. While his situation didn't compare to the size of a man's penis, public humiliation is corrosive and eats away at your self-confidence.

"Her version of the escapade was all over the locker room and campus by half-time. Students went from feeling sorry for her to busting his chops." Zende screeched to a halt on the keyboard and pointed a long finger at Reese. "You gotta know Noori's been keeping tabs on you."

After numerous years in the recording industry, Reese knew celebrity sexual dysfunction promoted the music more than the highest-priced advertising agency. "Why mess with me? There's lots of outrageous people in the artistic community. If your music is on point, what happens in your bedroom is nobody's business."

"The combination of musicians and church is explosive. Both are performance driven. One is open, and the other is closed, judgmental, and ruthless when the leader could be a player on either team." Zende could find a conspiracy theory anywhere.

"What's her point in conning me? I'm nobody." Reese acted as if he was finally wrapping his mind around the potential of Noori's calculated deception. "My wake-up call should have been her association with The International Truth Institute. They put out lies and distortions without any basis in fact. I didn't believe she was capable of twisting our relationship for her own purposes."

"Hustlers come in all forms, all ages and from all walks of life. Nobody knows what motivates them to cheat and con people?" Zende's fingers stilled. "They manipulate facts to suit their purposes. You need to figure out why you're on her radar screen. And why she pointed me in your direction? Maybe she's calculating a scandal surrounding your relationship with

Kamilah. There's lots of ca-ching from an explosive sexual tell-all."

CHAPTER FOURTEEN: REESE

REESE LEAPED UP, went to his credenza and pulled out a stack of ten by twelve-inch brown envelopes. He thrust the packets toward Zende. "Since you've come up with this epiphany, you might as well read what she sends to me cause I sure as hell don't go on her website."

Zende looked from the envelopes to Reese. Lines of confusion marred his forehead.

"Read them. Noori's taken every scientific and psychological advance about sexuality, homosexuality, and gender identity made in the last fifty years and reduced them to trite garbage and pseudo-science. She finds the one grain of information capable of being misconstrued, re-edited, or remade to create doubt and mislead the reader."

Zende sorted the large brown envelopes by date, opened them, and pulled out the articles one by one. Zende's eyes darkened and narrowed to slits as he scanned the titles. His mouth opened and closed like a fish out of water. "Why is she sending you this filthy shit?" Zende rubbed his shaking hands across his face.

"The commentaries come marked private, to be opened only by the addressee. I can't figure out what game she's playing. We aren't friends, but I'm not her enemy. Other than you and Milah, no one knows about our relationship which she ended."

Zende gulped. "It can't be good. She's invested a lot of time and energy on this…" he pointed a shaky hand at the essays, "trying to provoke you." Zende scanned more articles, his jaw tightening, his brow becoming a thundercloud as he read additional offensive comments. "You've got to figure out her agenda."

Reese had spent countless hours analyzing each one of the messages, praying to God about the looming nightmare. He believed in malevolent spirits, and Noori was one of them. "She's twisted up like a pretzel. These articles were written by someone living in a self-imposed twilight zone where they expect the irrational to return the world to the beginning of the twentieth century."

"Damn! Man, this is cruel and depraved." Zende threw the commentaries down on the table as if touching them was distasteful. He punched at a phantom enemy before returning to the papers.

Reese wandered around the studio, stopping from time to time to mutter under his breath. "She's one of Satan's imps prowling, out to devour me."

Zende ran the cold bottle across his forehead. "What did you do to piss her off?" Zende's voice dropped into the frigid zone.

"Dude, when I called Noori from the hospital, she wasn't into me. I never called again." Reese hissed, dragging his hands through his short hair. "She's the one making the overtures."

"I rarely repeat gossip, but there's something wrong with her head." Zende drank from the long-necked bottle of beer. Burped. "This confirms a lot of rumors about Noori. You left an impression on sistah girl."

Reese flipped Zende the bird. "She was wary, watchful and withdrawn when we were out in public. She couldn't keep her hands off me when we were alone."

"This is a twisted person turning a knife in someone's eye. Is she threatening you or trying to extort money?" Zende's body was taut now, his composure cracking as he perused the most recent article.

Reese sucked in a deep breath. "It's bizarre. Noori calls here. To the casual observer, she sounds friendly. She doesn't mention the articles that bash trans people... openly calling for violence and murder of people like me. If I didn't know better,

I'd say she was two people in one body." He was glad to have someone to unburden himself to. Finally.

"You have to do something about this." Zende passed one of the articles back to him.

Reese barely skimmed the title. Bile rose in his throat remembering the implied message. "What do you suggest? I should have listened to my sister and resigned last fall as planned. All I've worked for is on the line because of one crazy woman and a group of dumb-ass deacons."

Zende looked him up and down and jeered, "Is she afraid you'll out her? You slept together for months. Or is this revenge for you going through with the surgery?"

"Noori instigated our sexual interactions and controlled the places of our meetings."

"Think on this. Her parents were pressing her to get married. She was terrified of what she felt for you." Zende was derisive. "The marriage didn't last. She's bitter, and you're a convenient target. This vendetta isn't professional. If it were, she wouldn't be sending you brown envelopes. You'd be Exhibit A on The Truth Institute website. This is personal."

Reese dropped his head.

Zende slumped in his seat, shaking his head from side to side. "She knows what she's doing. She's playing you."

CHAPTER FIFTEEN:
ZENDE

BACK IN HIS GENERIC corporate condo with commercial oatmeal colored furnishings designed for high volume traffic, Zende's stomach was twisted in an origami knot. He didn't appreciate being used. Obviously, Noori had done her research, including Reese's Bermuda connections and placed Zende and the Thompkins together in Hamilton. Bermuda's capital city was home to little more than 1,000 people. Including his relationship with Kamilah. Frightening. She could have used the information in multiple ways. He needed time to assimilate the ramifications of this expanded knowledge.

The sicko had a bigger agenda. Noori believed she had access to rain down fire and brimstone on Reese. Punching in Noori's number and listening to her honeyed hello, he wanted to pour battery acid down her throat the same way she downed those Long Island Ice Teas. "Who set you up as Reese Thompkins' judge, jury, and executioner?"

"My research deals only with facts." Noori's voice was clipped, sliding into the East coast accent she'd perfected at Brown when other students laughed at her Midwest twang.

He heard the lie sliding off her forked tongue. Noori must have assumed he was an effing idiot or Reese wouldn't share the inflammatory messages.

"I'm looking at your uptight professional picture, your initials, and married surname." Reese didn't deserve this backstabbing, greedy bitch grabbing him by his nonexistent balls.

Noori's voice was placatingly sugary sweet. "The Institute pays me to write propaganda. I'm earning more money than if I was teaching at some second-rate university or begging for foundation research grants."

"When is it enough money, gurl?" Zende's question was rhetorical.

"Mr. Lightbourn, it's a dog-eat-dog world out there. We make choices." Her voice climbed two octaves into a sneer. "Reese Thompkins and his kind are in league with the devil."

Zende's mind pictured the green slime prevalent on children's game shows oozing out of her mouth. "While you and your daddy rail against the sinners who need the HIV drugs, you don't mind profiting from their misery." This act was a modern day take on a pact with the devil. "Gurl, I'm so pissed right now if you were in the room, I'd wring your chicken neck like the women used to do on the island. Snap your neck with one twist and let the blood drain out of the body until dead."

"Gross. You have the ammunition to get Kamilah out of there before the shit hits the fan. You should be thanking me." Her demented laugh cackled through the airwaves.

"My relationship with Kamilah has never been your concern."

"She's collateral damage." Noori paused. "You were nice to me at Brown. Most people weren't."

"Don't delude yourself. You did this for selfish reasons." He moved his shoulders and shifted his stance to alleviate the growing sense of menace. "You've put yourself in the same category as Stacy Dash, Don Lemon, and Juan Williams: sell-outs for a few dollars. Prostituting your expensive education by capitalizing on the ability to twist facts for the master."

"The Truth Institute will never bow to pressure or special interest groups. We operate according to God's Word. Nothing can be added or subtracted. The homosexual lifestyle has taken over the music industry. Have you gone over to the other side, too?"

"Daddy's money and poison did a slow but thorough job on you. You don't even sound like the woman I had dinner with recently. You used to have more self-respect."

"Being progressive, open, and understanding got me nowhere, either at home or in the workplace. Who speaks for God's side? Noori's laugh was high pitched and cruel. "The black community needs to be enlightened. They can choose to believe something other than what the preacher shouts from the pulpit on Sunday morning or across the Word Network. My parents believe in me, in what I'm doing. They paid for my education, not the government."

"One last question." Zende's voice dropped to a raspy whisper, "Exactly how did you conveniently remember Kamilah when you and I haven't spoken in years?"

"Information is power. You never know when it's going to come in handy." She disconnected the call.

Fuming, he punched in the phone number of a highly professional, Los Angeles-based private investigation firm. A confident voice said, "How can I help you?"

"Diamond, I need a thorough background check ... ASAP."

CHAPTER SIXTEEN:
REESE

O N THIS SUNDAY MORNING, God's people needed an encouraging message. It was hard to hear *O taste and see that the* LORD *is good: blessed is the man that trusted in Him* when the snow, which began on New Year's Eve continued every day since and the weatherman forecasted no relief in sight. Although the community was used to blizzards and long winters, they were still traumatized by the effects of last fall's tornado. The local FEMA coordination was caught up in bureaucratic red tape. Everywhere they looked, houses with tarps for roofs and doors wired shut were targets for vandalism and animals seeking shelter. The numbers of members and non-members asking for prayer and financial assistance increased daily. Those living in the campus housing had nowhere else to go.

Fighting through the concerns of his flock, Pastor Reese contemplated Noori Sherman's determination to use any weapon at her disposal to bring about his downfall. Parachuting Zende back into their lives fully opened his eyes. There wasn't any doubt about her motives. After prayer and devotions with his clergy team, Reese ascended the stairs to the pulpit. His eyes were drawn to a face he'd dreamt about. Annorah Sherman was seated in the front center section where Reese couldn't help but notice her as he approached the lectern. In the first-year post-surgery, Reese envisioned the woman sitting there where he could smile at her as he preached. He'd imagined feeling her love and support reflected at him.

She watched him with flat eyes like a coiled serpent ready to strike. Bile rose in his throat, and he swallowed it down. Now, looking at her reptilian face, his hands shook with the negative possibilities of her presence here. Reese shoved his hands in the pockets of the indigo robe to stop their trembling and moved away from the podium, relying on the lapel microphone for volume. He didn't intend to deviate from his planned text. His message was one of hope, of God's calling to all men. As he spoke, his voice calmed, and he moved into communing with God and his congregation. His eyes searched for Kamilah in her regular seat. Since she'd never met Noori, she had no idea a serpent was in their midst. Zende was seated with the musicians and focused on the sounds.

The Lord is amid His chosen people. The Lord is in the middle of His selected people during seasons of doubt, discomfort, and delay. We are His chosen people. He resides in our hearts. He loves us enough to set expectations; to urge us to do what is right; to tell us what is displeasing to Him; to chastise us. Those He loveth He chastises. He wants us to be spirit-filled—recognize sin, atone for our sins, and lean on Him.

Reese relied on examples of heroism to let the people see God working with them through their current situation. "There's food and shelter for all of our community. Our children have activities to keep their minds off when they're moving back into their homes. And for the parents, the public and private schools have reopened." At the conclusion of service, Reese gave the benediction and moved down the steps to confront Noori. His passage was blocked by Genesis who pushed the envelope crammed with bills into his hand.

"Here's the money she said I owe you." She tossed her head at Kamilah who was walking toward them. "I ain't sorry about nothing I did. If you would talk to me, you'd know what's waiting for you."

"Genesis, stop it." Kamilah put a restraining hand on the girl's arm.

98

The teen flipped her hair at Kamilah and faced Reese, keeping her voice low but threatening. "Me and my girls talk about sex. Not all men want a virgin. I figure if I get some experience, you might be more interested since it's clear yo wife can't even have a baby. You been married for five years. I can do what she obviously can't." Genesis stuck out her tongue at Kamilah. "I see her looking at the pregnant women with her cow eyes and trying to love up on every new baby in the congregation."

That little monster-in-training pricked Kamilah's Achilles' heel. Milah wanted children. Another thing they had not factored into this charade. Two years had become three, now five.

Reese gritted his teeth, praying no one was ear-hustling or watching this episode. "Genesis, stop disrespecting Kamilah. You think this is a game where you get together with your friends and figure out the most stupid thing you can do to get my attention. It doesn't work like that."

"All" and she stressed A L L "men are dogs. My mama said so. And besides, with that bad leg, I can take her in a fight." The heifer rocked her neck.

"Little girl, let's see what you made of." Kamilah walked into Genesis' face and hissed, "Repeat it."

Genesis, taken aback by Kamilah's words, backed away and ran off to join her crew.

By the time Reese had been stopped by a couple of dozen members with holy handshakes, requests for prayer, and pats on the back, Noori had vanished.

At 11:37 p.m. the tablet Reese kept on the bedside table beeped signaling an incoming message. Reese sat up in bed, turned on the nightlight, and opened the communication.

Truth Blog:

Pastor Reese Thompkins preaches all are welcome in God's house. Included in Thompkins' definition of ALL are fornicators, homos, he/shes. I read in the Bible where Jesus ran the money changers out of the temple because they defiled it. Scripture says: And Jesus entered the temple of God and cast out all them selling and buying in the temple, and overthrew the tables of the moneychangers, and the seats of them that sold the doves.

This researcher made an impromptu, unannounced visit to The Cathedral in Washington, Illinois as part of our ongoing research against blasphemers and witnessed the following selling and buying in the temple:

Selling food. There's a café with seating for two hundred, selling the best caramel macchiato coffee outside of Starbucks. However, no drinks are permitted in the sanctuary.

Bookstore. First Lady Kamilah Thompkins is a best-selling Christian author. You can purchase autographed copies of her books there. Don't forget to pick up an assortment of worship texts for congregants to learn the principles espoused by Pastor Reese. Not all of them are scripturally based.

CDs and videos of his sermons. The first propaganda machine for new converts and saints who don't take the time to read the Word of God. Personally, I support the King James Version.

CDs and DVDs of concerts performed by the Gospel Choir, Pastor Reese's handpicked traveling musical group. He's become a multi-millionaire as the promoter of the troupe. Quite a lucrative sideline for a man with a mega-congregation.

An assortment of secular items that could easily be purchased in Barnes and Noble or your local independent bookseller. Jesus would have a field day in the bookstore. Money changers. Signs saying, we accept debit, credit, check, and cash.

And if the rest of you clergy and laypersons can live with commerce because your church is doing the same thing, take a long hard look at who is inside the beautifully appointed sanctuary. Same-sex couples are worshipping alongside impressionable young people. We will never forsake the homosexual agenda when our children are told "God knew you before He formed you in your mother's womb. God loves you unconditionally. And don't let anyone tell you anything different." Wink. Wink.

We will never create enduring marriages between a man and a woman when single women with children are given positions of leadership in the church. Two women, and I won't mention any names, were flaunting their sexual prowess as they led the congregation in devotions. Exactly whose house is this, Pastor Reese?

Reese's icy fingers reached for the phone and punched in the numbers he couldn't erase from his brain.

The couple was in the middle of passionate foreplay before the second sexual romp when the phone pinged. Noori glanced at the screen and giggled. *Good. Message delivered.* Three more phone calls in rapid succession left her shaken to her core. She pushed at her partner's chest and rolled out of bed. "You need to leave."

Following her out of bed, Lyn's firm hands reached out to caress her stiff back. "Come back to bed. I'm just getting revved up."

Noori wriggled out of Lyn's grasp and reached for the robe she'd carelessly tossed on the end of the bed. She pulled it around her and tied the sash. Pushing back her hair Lyn's hands had wrapped around her fingers a few minutes earlier,

Noori looked at Lyn's frustrated face. "I made a mistake. This … can't continue."

The other woman backed away. "No problem, baby girl. I know a whole lot of women who want what I can offer." Lyn kissed her forehead. "Whoever she is, she's messed you up for anyone else. However, when you change your mind, I'll be there for you."

Once Lyn left, Noori took a long hot shower and then sat in her much-loved chair staring out into the darkness. Tears rolled down her cheeks. When would she stop acting irrationally where Rielle was concerned? Returning from the impulsive visit, she'd lied to her father about needing to work, gone into her office, written the blog, and set the automatic timer for it to be delivered to Rielle at the same time it went public. Then she'd gone to A10 for a late dinner rather than go home to an empty condo. Lyn was in her usual spot at the end of the bar. Alone. In a weak moment, Noori accepted Lyn's invitation to join her for dinner and drinks. One thing led to another, and they ended up smoking a blunt together and falling into Noori's bed—ravishing each other's naked bodies until Reese's incessant phone calls interrupted them.

Noori pulled a bottle of Jameson from the side table and drank directly from the bottle. "I'm not a freak; I like men... I'm not a freak... I like men." She took another drink, repeating "I like men... I'm not a freak..."

CHAPTER SEVENTEEN: REESE

BEFORE DAYLIGHT MONDAY MORNING, Reese had left a dozen unanswered requests for Noori to call him. His sleep was interrupted by the acid buildup and wild dreams playing out in his head. What psychotic game was she playing? Siccing Zende on Kamilah. Showing up at Sunday services. Reese showered, dressed, cancelled the staff meeting, and drove his Land Rover to the offices of The International Truth Institute in Evanston, Illinois.

Noori's assistant made several calls after Reese refused to leave without talking to her boss. He shook his head at the blond, blue-eyed Jesus, prominently framed with a small light adding a glow to his face. Books and magazines scattered around the two small tables next to the chairs were little more than propaganda pieces for the right. The assistant finally got through to her employer. She directed Reese to Noori's parents' home.

He leaned on the doorbell, hearing the loud peals through the door, and waited. In springtime, it was probably a lovely setting. Dr. Thaddeus Sherman's pale eyes bugged out when he opened the door. "Hello... I'm Reese Thompkins."

"We know who you are." Dr. Sherman spat out the words through gritted teeth. Speaking of a royal "we" even though the two men were alone in the doorway. "You the one praying for the anti-Christ to come. What do you want?"

The anti-Christ. A strangely apocalyptic statement even for Dr. Sherman. The negative comments Noori made about her father came flooding back. His mantra was we are living in the end times. Christ is soon to return. He was homophobic, rigidly religious, setting unrealistic standards of perfection for her and her two brothers.

"Her administrate assistant said I could find Noori here." Reese looked beyond Dr. Sherman into the foyer with parquet floors where birds-of-paradise flowers were meticulously arranged in a cut-glass bowl sitting atop a round pedestal table. The man made no motion for him to come in out of the frigid wind.

"Voncile said you were on your way over here." Dr. Sherman's voice snapped like a whip. "You want to beat up on Noori for proudly proclaiming God's Word like she's been taught since a little girl."

No doubt Dr. Sherman had read his daughter's latest blog. When they were a couple, Noori revealed her conflicted views of her parents. She would imitate the man's words, precise King's English at the office and country as cornbread and buttermilk fresh from the milking cow at home. His disgust and anger were directed at poor black folks, "hood rats and thugs" who ought to be doing more than having babies, selling drugs, and going to jail. Both parents parroted the harsh words of the white people they worked and socialized with. Dr. Sherman was out-of-touch with the daily struggles of his poverty-stricken relatives or the men he'd grown up with who were caught up in the school to prison pipeline. It was his way or the highway.

Reese rubbed his cold hands together while holding on to his temper. "Sir, this is a private matter between your daughter and me. Is she here or not?"

Dr. Sherman frowned at Reese, his heavy-set body barring the younger man from entering the house. "Who the hell are you to barge into my house and demand anything?"

WINTER'S LAMENT

"I'm freezing in your doorway while you're carrying on an inquisition. Can I speak to Noori?" *Puh-leeze. What happened to civility and common courtesy?*

Sherman did not move.

Reese pressed the hostile man for a response. "She's harassing me. She's openly vilifying my ministry. Can you tell her I'm here?"

"Noori's got nothing to say to the likes of you." Dr. Sherman studied the cars moving slowly up the street, apparently not listening to anything about his daughter's defaming, disingenuous campaign to humiliate Reese Thompkins.

On a couple of occasions, Noori's fury boiled over when her father's sour talk slandered the gay children of family members, friends, and coworkers. These family and friends were not welcome in their home, and she was not to socialize with them. Dr. Sherman denigrated President Obama for not being black enough, for being a Muslim while pretending to be a Christian, for embracing the homosexual agenda, for refusing to support the Defense of Marriage Act, and for letting gays serve openly in the military.

Dr. Sherman's face contorted with rage. He slammed the door in Reese's face.

CHAPTER EIGHTEEN: NOORI

AFTER HER LOUSY NIGHT, Noori went to an Alcoholics Anonymous meeting. Not the one with her father's snitch, but one closer to her Hyde Park condo. For an hour, she reflected on the downward spiral of her life. She'd lost her sobriety coin. She hadn't been able to make it one week without a drink, much less thirty days.

Back in her home office, she sat in front of the computer screen, updating her information on the naked preacher whose fabrications were convincing enough to make someone take the picture down from the Internet. The unlucky pastor didn't know the woman he cut loose in exchange for keeping his pulpit and access to his wife's family's wealth had delivered the roll of film to Noori. Noori's assignment was to make sure each word hit below the kneecaps, undercutting his good works, and weakening his ministry.

Her corkboard held incriminating pictures of the research targets: megachurch leaders from across the United States. Homosexuals. Pedophiles. Thieves. Con artists. A Murderer. Each one had a secret, but none as jaw-dropping as Pastor Reese Thompkins. She kept her documentation here in a locked file cabinet. She didn't have confidence in her Truth Institute colleagues any more than they trusted her.

Thaddeus Sherman's blustering voice cut into Noori's musing. "That visit was a dumb-ass move even the lowliest poker player wouldn't make. What are you doing—tipping your hand before The Institute's plan is ready to roll out?" Her father had let himself into the condo with his key and pounced on her.

Her lapse in judgment along with Reese's late-night phone messages shook her, forcing her to rethink how easy outing him would be. Noori wasn't equipped to fight with this new Reese, an unyielding Reese, not the love-struck tranny willing to do anything to gain a few crumbs of affection. And Noori was having a harder time fighting herself. Two dozen red roses were delivered to the apartment this morning with a note… "I'm available Whatever you need—whenever. Thanks for a fascinating evening… until next time. L." Noori knew she should've thrown them in the trash, but they were an exquisite dark red, velvety against white baby's breath, adding fragrance to the room and lightening her depression.

"We're this close to wrapping up this exposé on pastors and the homosexual agenda with Reese Thompkins as the primary example. I've got personal money and influence riding on this deal." Thaddeus frowned, wrinkled his nose. "Why the hell did you tell Voncile you were working at my house? I've warned you about missing work, turning in projects after the deadline." He scrutinized the space and her in lounging pajamas and a robe. "Are you on a drinking binge?"

She looked up at him, then away. "Daddy, you told me not to tell anyone I was attending AA meetings. I can't just disappear. If they believe I'm working at your place, it's easier all around." Although it was true today, she'd been holding the lie in her pocket for a while now. If he and Voncile never conferred about her whereabouts, she was on safe ground.

"Okay, this time. But why was Thompkins looking for you in the first place?"

"He wasn't responding to the letters or the articles." Noori didn't mention the periodic phone calls she made to him. Her voice was hesitant, unsure. "How was I supposed to know he'd go ballistic over a blog post?"

His timely phone call stopped you from compounding another blunder. You don't play with women like Lyn and walk away unscathed.

107

You need to get rid of those roses before you get caught up in some romantic fog and invite her to come over again.

Thaddeus swung her chair around to face him, stooping down into her personal space. "Don't mess this up with liquor clouding your brain, girl? You strolled into The Cathedral as if you were some slut." He gave her knees a quick hurtful squeeze. He had a wicked light in his eyes. "He came by the house looking for you. Do you hear me?"

"No one recognized me except Thompkins." Noori sucked in a deep cleansing breath. "I should've sat in the balcony, but—"

Her father grabbed her arms, shaking her like Raggedy Ann. She saw hatred in his sherry-colored eyes and didn't know if it was directed at Reese, or her, or both. "But you wanted that demon to see you."

Noori tried to appease her father. "I wanted to rattle Thompkins and demonstrate I could get in his face at any time." She jerked away from her benefactor, but he was holding her wrists.

"Why, Noori? Why now? Our plan to elevate the truth depends on secrecy and stealth. When we pounce, we want it to be reminiscent of dropping bombs on Hiroshima, Japan, leaving nothing and no one untouched. Something people will remember fifty years later."

CHAPTER NINETEEN:
REESE

ONCE DR. SHERMAN SLAMMED the door in his face, Reese refused to waste the day's trip to Chicago. Although Rev. Thornton was a competent second-in-command, Reese decided to make cold calls on three music producers the Gospel Choir worked with in the past to follow-up on written pitches he'd made regarding support for the Tower rebuilding. He left two companies with sizeable checks while the third company agreed to present the proposal to their charitable contributions department. Reese also received two additional leads of Christian media outlets who were looking for markets in Central and downstate Illinois.

Reese chuckled to himself over the unexpected consequences of the deacons' meddling. The press releases, pledge cards and Internet hook-up were in place. Media attention Reese hadn't counted on afforded his fundraising efforts a huge boost. Monetary donations poured in from unsolicited sources. Some donors requested specific prayers. Businesses asked to be connected to the ministry. The current total was $3.2 million and rising daily.

After his final appeal for money, Reese drove around the nation's Second City, revisiting the places he and Noori had frequented. He drove past the apartment where she used to live. No longer distracted by the lust-filled memories of an inexperienced lover, the interactions seemed calculated instead of spontaneous. Unable to make sense of the past colliding with the present, Reese called his former therapist, briefly told her the facts, and begged her to fit him in this evening. She agreed.

Dr. Luna Erickson was a Swedish blonde, built like a linebacker and stood six feet tall. Her partner taught women's studies at another university. Together they had been writing, publishing, speaking out forcefully on discrimination based on sexual identity and sexual orientation. Her private practice was located on the third floor of an old Hyde Park commercial building. She offered him a seat on the green and blue patterned couch and sat in the comfortable coordinated blue armchair across from him. The setting took him back to the fifteen months of intensive therapy, the numerous hours he spent peeling back the veil of his history as though it were an onion. His sexual preferences. His sexual identity. Convincing this therapist, he was a man trapped in a woman's body.

"Thanks for seeing me, Doc." Reese shook hands with the noted scholar and activist. "After all these years, Noori Sherman has put a bullseye on my chest" He jumped right into the issue, knowing her dislike of small talk.

Dr. Erickson snapped, "I'm angry to hear you've been in ongoing contact with Dr. Sherman. Her current research and writings on sexuality and sexual identity are opposite to the position we teach at the university."

"Back then, Dr. Sherman, … Noori and I were friends." Reese's eyes skittered away, and he homed in on the framed pictures, degrees, and certificates on the walls, anywhere he could hide. He looked down at his hands clenching the arms of the chair, "… more like lovers."

Her blue eyes were colder than the high winds rolling off frozen Lake Michigan. She opened her mouth, then closed it for several minutes. "I've been doing this work long enough to know patients don't always do what they're supposed to do." Dr. Erickson's clipped words retained traces of the Scandinavian accent she'd never entirely lost. "Was this going on while you were in therapy?"

"Yeah." He experienced the same shame when Poppi told him to study his spelling words and instead he played his music, flunking numerous spelling tests.

Doc rolled her eyes at him. "Tell me the whole truth." Her harsh voice cut through Reese's apologies.

Sitting up straighter and squaring his shoulders, the repentant preacher divulged it all. He stopped twice to get bottles of water from the mini fridge she kept at the back of the office. Based on Dr. Erickson's lack of reaction, the whole account sounded sordid. Like having an affair while in a committed relationship with someone else.

"Over the nine months, you didn't meet any of the significant people in her life." The psychiatrist zeroed in on his weak denials of personal blame. Dr. Erickson had staked her reputation on what he shared with her during therapy. He felt worse than gangrenous puss oozing out of an infected leg.

She snorted, "Most of the people who espouse what I call the made-up Bible-based rhetoric are educated at Christian colleges." Her venom turned to her former intern. "You can't turn on these televangelist stations without hearing twenty-four hours non-stop of these preachers advocating killing gay or trans people without any fear of moral judgment."

Reese dropped his head. He encountered these men and women, not on television, but in his daily association with fellow clergy.

"My intuition tells me Annorah entered into the relationship with ulterior motives." She tapped her chin and jotted down some notes. When she looked up at him, she prodded him. "Something must have changed for her to continue this association with you."

He slapped his forehead. Without the fantasy world he'd created, what remained was a charade, a grimy back-alley affair. Noori had manipulated him, laughed at him. God, he'd been a dupe, starved for someone to love him. He didn't hear from her again until he was installed as senior pastor at The Cathedral.

"You didn't fit her preconceptions about a transgendered person." Dr. Erickson opened a file and shared the photos she'd taken of him when she began treating him. "Even without the surgery and enhancements, you presented as a metrosexual male. But she couldn't take the chance of someone inadvertently outing you." Dr. Erickson exhaled. "A woman-slash-man preparing to complete the physical transition. You must have rocked her world." She mumbled.

His heart seized. He wanted to scream out loud about the pain of the deception and how it had affected him going forward.

The doctor's words brought him back. "Your relationship took her out of her comfort zone." Dr. Erickson pushed her chair back, stood and walked to the window to stare out onto the busy street where cars and pedestrians were stuck in the last of the rush hour traffic.

Reese looked at his watch. Over two hours had passed while they dissected his mess.

Dr. Erickson uttered a harsh expletive. "My colleagues and I used to laugh about Bible thumpers who refused to expand their horizons. They couldn't see value in the science when it didn't square with their God created the world in seven days. God created Adam and Eve; not Adam and Steve."

Leaving her to ponder, he gazed around the room, comforted to know this haven was here for trans people seeking acceptance in a world continuously bent on finding new ways to discriminate against them.

"Annorah' s slapping at you now is about her own repressed sexuality." Dr. Erickson hunched her shoulders and turned back to him.

In his prayer talks with God, this was the one scenario he'd never considered. "If she'd face me instead of this malicious game, I'd have a better idea of what I'm up against."

"Whatever her endgame, it is filthy. The most offensive part is her obscenities are creating havoc at a time when the psychiatric community is making remarkable strides in the sexual identity arena." Reese paid meticulous attention to the fear-mongering on the political right. "They lump all sexual politics together. Pedophilia, transvestites, gay, and transgendered are characterized as the so-called homosexual agenda. Fundamentalist preachers and their followers have gotten stronger over the years and are spouting a form of bigotry equating homosexuality with giving one's self over to Satan. There's no coming back unless the person is cured of homosexuality by God and one of their Christian counselors."

Her analysis choked him. Reese uttered the words immediately as they formed in his mind. "Can you check your records to see if she might have scammed other patients?"

"Give me a second." Dr. Erickson walked to her desk, sat down, and turned on her computer, entered a few keystrokes and waited for the files to pop up. Shock and horror flitted across her face. "During the time Annorah interned here, there were four cases of Body Dysmorphic Disorder or BDD, where she completed the psycho-social study." BDD is listed in APA as a mental disorder characterized by an obsessive preoccupation with some aspect of one's own appearance that is severely flawed and warrants exceptional measures to hide or fix it.

He'd read a copy of the psycho-social report and Dr. Erickson's analysis which were forwarded to the Belgrade gender reassignment clinic. "The words Noori wrote in response to the interviews she conducted were the ticket to your acceptance of me as a patient and ultimately my freedom."

The therapist, reading from the screen, shared, "One of the patients was a middle-aged man, married with children, who identified as female. He underwent surgery shortly before you did. The other two cases were like yours, female to male, although both were white."

"Do you think I'm the only one she's stalking?" Either way, he'd been used for her twisted pleasure.

Dr. Erickson pushed her large hands through her white-blonde hair. He imagined her wrapping those blunt fingers around Noori's neck and squeezing. A measure he'd employ if she'd conned him from the beginning, deceived him and played with his emotions. Dr. Erickson asked, "Have you considered pressing charges against her?"

"Could this have been a long con? Not me, but this issue." Conspiracy theories were the lifeblood of theatre folk. Noori reminded him of method actors, actors who became the part. Studied the person they were to portray in minute detail until it was hard to know the difference between reality and fantasy.

Dr. Erickson blinked. "Annorah Sherman asked to intern with me specifically. She came to a symposium where I was the featured presenter and asked provocative questions. I was impressed with her depth of knowledge about my research. She'd read all my papers and my dissertation."

"Did she seem skeptical?"

The psychiatrist's eyebrows raised as if questioning her own objectivity. "Reese, we have to get the university involved in this. The administration will skin me alive if they learn I had damming information regarding a noted graduate of our program who is philosophically opposed to our beliefs and patient interaction. Her ulterior motives might spill over on the university."

"Can't we handle this quietly, without getting the university involved?"

Erickson tapped her screen where the three other names were visible. "Reese, we'll handle the internal investigation discreetly. All Ph.D. students enrolled in the Psychology Department are required to spend a year in personal therapy with an APA approved therapist. Dr. Warren was the analyst while Annorah was in the program. I'll have a conversation with her."

"I'm sorry Dr. Erickson. I believed she cared about me." Knowing his apology was insufficient, he offered it anyway.

Her lips twisted in a wry smile that didn't reach her eyes, "Patients often experience transference of feelings and desires toward the therapist. I wish you'd told me sooner... about the time your feelings changed from professional to personal."

"If I'd had any idea it would come to this, I would have." He stood, walked over, and retrieved his coat.

"We're going to have to determine if Annorah is up to something more sinister." Dr. Erickson held out her hand to him. "When APA declared homosexuality no longer a mental illness; when states stopped criminalizing homosexual behavior, it was largely due to activism on the part of the gay community. This window of opportunity to have more people interested in this work is too important to allow an unethical practitioner to taint it. One way or another, Annorah Sherman will have to publicly answer for her actions."

CHAPTER TWENTY:
NOORI

AFTER YEARS OF ON-AGAIN and off-again inpatient and outpatient treatment, Noori was a functional alcoholic. Reese's visit, her tryst with Lyn, daddy-dumbest' s threats tipped her fragile control, and she spent the day drinking while intermittently working at her home office desk. Shortly before 10 p.m. that evening, Noori finally sobered up enough to attempt some damage control. She punched in Reese's number and thumped on the desk until he answered. "What was the purpose of the stunt you pulled, Thompkins?" Noori sounded haughty and victimized in the same breath. "Going to my parents' home. Involving them in a private matter." She placed the phone on speaker and got up to prowl around her exquisitely furnished master bedroom, taking large gulps from a highball glass of Jameson, neat. The half-empty bottle sat on her night table next to the roses.

Thompkins' voice held a gruffness she hadn't encountered before. "Call a halt to this harassment, Noori. Is this how the Truth Institute operates?"

Was he growing some balls at this late date? "Whoa, buddy." Daddy-dumbest had her on a short leash. There was money, notoriety, and vindication riding on this deal.

"You decided to turn up the heat when you didn't get the response you expected from the numerous threats you sent." Her nemesis' hollow voice filled the room, bouncing off the walls.

She paced the soft woolen carpeted floor, dragging her feet through the thick pile, horror-struck at the words pouring out of the phone. Her forehead throbbed. All she wanted to do was turn off the lights and lie down until her head stopped spinning.

"You showed up at The Cathedral and posted a piece of filth aimed directly at me on your blog the same day." Thompkins' voice was steely, chopping away at her. "Did you dictate the blog on your drive back to the city?"

Having ferreted out Zende was still hanging around The Cathedral, Noori had to know for sure if sparks were flying between the two rivals. Learning the intimate details of the two men's in-fighting was too private a matter to send someone else in to do surveillance. "Don't be so melodramatic." Her laughter sounded hysterical to her ears. The churning in her gut said she'd gone for the jugular when an ambush would have served her purposes better. Her shaking hand set the glass down next to the bottle.

Thompkins wanted a fight, and she had a career on the line. She needed a different strategy. She needed to shut him down. Quickly. "Juvenile thinking is what makes you so easy to figure out." She walked to the large window and looked out through snow-smattered surfaces, her hot breath leaving more spots on the glass panes.

"Noori, you blow up my phone. You spread filth over the Internet." He spoke as if she were that demented doll, Chuckie.

She itched to twist a hunting knife in his gut and watch him bleed out for being around to remind her of the worst error in judgment she'd made. "At least I didn't marry my sister." She'd relish punching him in his nose, breaking it, and messing up that smug chiseled face. "Incest is taboo! You ever read the Book of David?"

He sniffed. "... I'm sure that's your snide way of determining if I do read the Bible. The story is about David's son, Ammon, raping his sister, Tamar, and setting off a family war. The reference is found in Second Samuel, the thirteenth chapter."

Oh no! He had on his big boy pants today. This conversation had taken a left turn, in his direction. "Baaa—by, you're gonna raise my profile. I'm gonna be bigger than Oprah. Shit, I'm gonna be bigger than Michelle Obama when I lay your ass bare."

"What is this about, Noori?" The question was straightforward.

How could she have gotten so far off-track, so involved with such an unsuitable person? "I've seen you. You... lying ... manipulating piece of dog shit." The images burned into her head and her heart.

"I never lied to you."

"That is goin ta be your downfall." She had the facts from his lying mouth.

"Ah, Dr. Sherman... the law protects information gained from a private patient-therapist relationship."

Who the hell was he to be schooling her on the boundaries of their relationship? "But not when I'm working undercover." She had him where she wanted him. Scared. Defenseless. Pastor Reese Thompkins' deceptive lifestyle was her ticket to the big time.

"Huh? Our relationship was a part of your undercover assignment? How far will you descend into the pit of hell... sex and declarations of love...for the exposé?"

"As long as the facts are clear, morality is out of the equation. The money these people are paying me—"

"They weren't paying you when you slept with me." He cut her off.

"Back then you were nobody. With Bruce Jenner wavering with his transition, all this noise about how brave he is, how he's the face of the new protected class." She scoffed. "This is the perfect time to show you, a black female to male transition, and the rest of these perverts for the frauds you are."

"By doing this, you're outing yourself as well." Reese's voice was assertive.

"My involvement will be carefully edited out of the story." She wiped moisture from her top lip. "An investigator does what she has to."

"Get over yourself. I'm insulted by these ass wipes who promote you as if you're Mother Theresa."

Noori hadn't paid enough attention to the contemporary Reese. She'd underestimated him with the ill-advised visit and hastily written blog. Now his ego was engaged in a way it hadn't been before. *Damn!*

CHAPTER TWENTY-ONE: NOORI

THE CABLE NETWORK GREENLIGHTED The International Truth Institute's project for six guaranteed episodes and optioned another six segments based on the response to the first two shows. Ratings were everything on cable television. Old man Lord crowed, "That's twelve episodes because we know you gonna rock this." Lord and her father saw themselves as kingmakers and in her case, a queen. The two old fools would ride the wave until a new cause came along where the Institute could shine a spotlight on others who operated beneath their beliefs.

Yep. Reese Thompkins is gonna make me a household name.

Because Noori conceived, researched the series, and pitched it, she was the showrunner, the person in charge, the person responsible for creative direction and overseeing the project from start to finish. The network provided her with a team to create and revise scripts on the eleven stories, but the first story was hers alone. All staff signed airtight confidentiality agreements. Her national reputation was gonna be built on this exposé. And she was making sure no one knew the details until she revised history and erased every tidbit that might surface of her involvement.

"Thanks, guys. I've got my list of to dos, and we'll meet again in two weeks."

"Man, I love your new look, Dr. Sherman."

Gone were the braids replaced by a shorter hairstyle until closer to her debut. Based on all the testing and feedback, a look that closely resembled Tamron Hall was determined to be best for her. Noori was provided hours of footage to study Tamron Hall's work as a news anchor on MSNBC. The woman also covered hard news stories on *Investigation America* and *Deadline: Crime* on the Discovery Channel. Hall's documentaries had earned her numerous nominations and awards during her career. The investigative reporter stuck to the script. ALWAYS.

"Remember, we're going to the top, and you have to look the part. Your lunch is on the office desk. Hummus, raw veggies, and a protein shake. Water." The producer walked out the door leaving her to the asinine lunch. The company hired a personal trainer for their newest superstar-in-training and changed her diet to vegan. Because the cameras were unforgiving, she was rapidly dropping the weight and building muscle. If she could just give up the booze, everything would be fine.

Voncile rushed through the door opening before Noori would slam the door and get off a primal scream. "This certified letter was delivered by courier an hour ago. I had to sign for it, but I didn't open it." Noori's research was strictly confidential. As a new hire, Voncile was screamed at and threatened with termination for opening a piece of private mail concerning one of the preachers Noori was gathering filth about.

"Thanks, Voncile." Noori sat down, dismissing her assistant, and uncovered the unappetizing plate.

Voncile left, quietly closing the door behind her.

Noori kicked off the high heels. She was three inches shorter than Tamron Hall, and the producers were attempting to give her more height and stature. She unbuttoned the tight-assed collar of the expensive silk blouse she wore, a part of the new look designed to appeal to conservative audiences. Noori cringed inwardly at the university logo in the upper left-hand corner of the envelope. Noori withdrew the engraved letter opener her brothers presented to her when she was released from the Betty Ford Clinic. Inscribed on the handle were the words *opening a new chapter.*

Her eyes searched the one-page letter signed by the university's lawyer, Marc Hallstrom. She was facing ethics charges, and Reese Thompkins had lodged the complaint. Absently, she reached for a bottle she kept in the office. There was nothing there. Her father had threatened her again about not ruining his life's work. No alcohol. No missteps. Nothing anyone could use against her. Not even Dolton.

Noori threw her lunch at the wall. She picked up her phone and punched in the number. A barely recognizable voice answered. She screamed. "Don't congratulate yourself too soon, Thompkins. You'll wish you'd never slithered out from under that rock when I'm through with you."

CHAPTER TWENTY-TWO: REESE

REESE NAVIGATED THE Land Rover north on I-55 to Chicago for another meeting with the team Luna Erickson had assembled with the urgency of cleaning up this mess without public fallout for the university. Dr. Erickson's intern had violated the Code of Ethics by engaging in a sexual relationship with at least one of the patients she was assigned to work with.

Reese was accompanied by Kamilah and Zende who needed a 'date night.' The duo was taking baby steps toward a permanent reconciliation. Their love was apparent to him although they were careful to avoid bringing attention to themselves. In public settings around The Cathedral, they were old friends catching up after a long absence. Within the sanctuary of his and Kamilah's apartment, the lovers kept public displays of affection to a minimum. Reese felt their pain and dropped them off at the W Hotel to give them time alone to sort out their plans.

The Ethics Committee meeting was being held in the university's legal department's conference room complete with dark flocked walls, bookcases, and dark Asian tables. The minimal color in the room was provided by white chairs and Lake Michigan seascapes on the walls. The seascapes reminded him of God's omnipresence. *God's got me. No matter what Noori does, I will not allow her to get away with slander and half-truths.*

Chairman Hallstrom opened the committee meeting with introductions, the purpose of the committee, and anticipated outcomes. Given the nature of the charges and the reputations of all parties involved, Hallstrom stressed the need for complete confidentiality. A stenographer, poised to record the meeting, sat away from the team. Once the opening remarks concluded, the chair called on Dr. Warren. "Dr. Zeline Warren was Annorah Sherman's university appointed therapist during her Ph.D. program. She will provide us with a profile of the accused to guide tonight's discussion."

"This profile is based on my notes from weekly interactions with Annorah Sherman throughout a calendar year plus the new information we received recently." Dr. Warren, a petite brown-skinned woman with Bantu twists and wire-rimmed glasses, sat at the right end of the conference table. She spoke from a set of prepared notes. She spoke at length concluding with "Except for the gender identity issue, Reese Thompkins possessed the personal characteristics Dr. Sherman valued in a relationship."

"Speak in plain English," The chair demanded, peering down at the massive file his staff had accumulated for the case. "The world is too complicated, and I'm an old-fashioned lawyer."

Dr. Warren nodded, "We're all colleagues here. Let me break it down for you. Reese Thompkins was handsome, smart, and talented. He believed he was born in the wrong body and sought out Dr. Erickson to help him get to the right body, so to speak."

Luna Erickson laughed. "I couldn't have articulated it better myself. He wanted to look like he felt and acted."

Dr. Warren studied the faces at the table and reminded them of what was at stake. "Our legal and medical system declared Reese had to live as a man for a year. Living as a man involves interaction with the opposite sex, taking on male roles and acknowledging his sexuality. Simultaneously, he'd undergo significant psychoanalysis and then if the stars aligned, he'd get his ticket punched for a new life in the body he desired."

"Sexual reassignment surgery." The chair crossed off the words scribbled on top of his files.

"Yes. Annorah Sherman complicates the plot line." Dr. Warren looked at Reese, giggled and wagged her pen at him. "She was supposed to spend four hours with you." She held up four fingers. "Collect specific information as required by the American Psychiatric Association and write a social history. Afterward, she was to submit a completed report to assist Luna Erickson with pinpointing the patient's needs for social and emotional support during the process and exit Stage Left."

"Four hours? Is that enough time to learn somebody's life story?" The chair sounded uncertain but added four hours to his notepad.

"With skill and diligence, a junior researcher can unearth the basics and provide the senior therapist with a framework to build on." Dr. Warren reminded him, "Reese was going to have weekly therapy sessions with Luna throughout the year."

"What else can you share about Dr. Sherman's temperament or judgment?" Levi Blumenthal, the university's ombudsman could best be described as rumpled. His dark hair was disheveled. His dark gray jeans, shirt, and jacket needed to be sent to the cleaners for refreshing. The ombudsman was there to protect the rights of Annorah Sherman as well as the rights of Reese and the two other men the committee's investigation discovered.

"She became cold and manipulative whenever we got too close to anything remotely real."

"Did Dr. Sherman have additional contact with the other dysphoria patients?", the university's watchdog asked.

The chair spelled out the results of the inquiry conducted by two senior members of the investigation firm the university used. "Yes. Both men have been deposed by the university's legal team but refused to appear before the committee or to confront Dr. Sherman in public. They value their privacy more than facing her again or being reminded of that time in their lives."

"In what way?"

The chair passed the ombudsman a client folder. "Case Number Two was suspicious during the second date following the conclusion of the formal assessment. He was living "La Vida Loco" since taking testosterone and facial enhancements had rendered him more masculine in appearance. Number Two wanted to show off that all kinds of women were into him to his skeptical friends and family. When Ms. Sherman hesitated for the second time about having Sunday dinner with his family, he cut her loose."

The watchdog perused the papers and looked up over his half glasses. "Hurray for him. He sounds like a stand-up guy. How's he doing?"

Luna Erickson interjected, "He's living with a woman, and saving up for the surgery. He was offered a chance to come in to talk about where he is in the process at no charge. We owed him that much for invading his privacy."

The chair pointed out, "If the charges are supported, and this goes to the APA, the three defendants are going to get more than a few free therapy sessions."

Zeline Warren pointed to herself, tapping her breastbone, nostrils flaring. "Annorah' insecurities about parental expectations and religious philosophy got in the way of connecting with her repressed sexuality." The psychoanalyst passed around a transcript of one session.

"Dr. Warren, did you learn anything useful?" The ombudsman asked.

"In her words, the woman's an amalgamation of judgmental Baptist, Methodist, and Pentecostal religious traditions. Her parents taught her to obey and all the other nonsense designed to control children's behavior. Her family believes you work hard so you can go to heaven and get the white robe and mansion you were denied on this earth because you were black."

Luna inserted, "It takes a critical thinker to balance the science, sexual dynamics and the fundamentalist church teachings on sex."

"Fundamentalists teach sex is only between a married man and his wife. Anything else is fornication. Fornicators are going to hell. Sodomy, bestiality, or homosexuality means you're going to hell with gasoline drawers," Warren sermonized. "The church wasn't dealing with transsexuals at all until recently."

"What happens next?" The ombudsman directed his question to the chair. He scribbled a few notes on a legal pad situated next to the materials provided to the committee members.

"Dr. Sherman will receive a copy of the charges. There will be a hearing. She'll have a right to her own counsel and a chance to tell her side of the story."

"Will I have to testify?" Reese's acid-filled stomach reminded him of what was at stake.

"Yes, Mr. Thompkins," the chair answered immediately. "If she denies the allegations or responds that you misread her intentions, you'll have to rebut her testimony."

Having spent his lifetime terrified of violence and of being murdered, Reese tried his best to control all interactions with other people. That was about to change. When he was outed, his celebrity would skyrocket. He'd be the flava of the month for a long while. The talk shows and televangelism's talking heads would ratchet up the debate over God's infallibility. Both groups would intentionally inflict more hatred on those who are born different.

CHAPTER TWENTY-THREE:
ZENDE

"Why hy you so covered up?" Zende wrapped his long arms around Kamilah to assist her in shedding her long black coat and an oversized hat covering her head and part of her face. without the coat, she revealed her beautiful body in skinny black jeans, angora turtleneck sweater and blazer. Heat simmered between them, and he was tired of pretending to be an old friend who was hanging around until his throat healed. He craved the touch of her smooth skin.

The Capital Grille on North Saint Clare was within walking distance of the W Hotel. It was an intimate restaurant with an exquisite menu and service. Zende had reserved a quiet table in the back of the restaurant where they'd have privacy. The discreet wait service stood a way off, waiting for them to settle in. He hung up her outer garment on the hook himself.

"It's windy and cold out there." Kamilah blew on her cold hands and rubbed them together before linking her hands together on top of the table's tablecloth.

He shifted in his seat until one of his hard thighs brushed her leg and settled against it. "We walked two blocks from the W to here." He placed his hands over hers, rubbing them until they were warm. He'd rather kiss them.

"Traveling incognito." She reminded him of Reese's request to stay low-key until he resolved this madness with

Noori. His students were pressing him to return to Boston to assist in their final programs prior to graduation.

A waiter interrupted the minor tiff. He placed the menus in front of them and explained the evening's specials before asking for their drink orders.

"Bring the lady a glass of your best champagne and I'll have a cola," Zende informed the older man without waiting for Kamilah to speak.

Milah shot him a tantalizing look and smiled up at the waiter, "I'll have a Sanford 201 Pinot Noir instead." She pinched the fleshy area of his arm with her thumb and forefinger.

Zende let go of the old Algonquin brave approach. It never worked before. The relationship was almost solidified, but they hadn't made any concrete plans yet. He nodded at the man. "How are the lobster tails?"

"Delivered fresh today, sir."

"Shouldn't your throat have been checked by now?" She checked him out rather than the menu selections.

"My surgeon renewed my prescriptions by phone. Tonight, it's about us and a little bit about Reese." He held her hand, making her shiver. Soon he'd be able to claim her publicly. "I invited someone to join us."

The waiter returned with their drinks. Zende placed their order for lobster and mac and cheese. Once the waiter left, they resumed their quiet conversation as a jazz trio and the clink of silverware muffled other diners' conversations.

A woman walked up to the table. "Am I intruding?" She was somewhere around fifty with beautiful dark skin, long curly hair, and wire-framed glasses. She wore an ankle length, dark burgundy merino wool coat, an infinity scarf and matching leather gloves.

"Diamond, you're a little early," Zende jumped up and hugged the woman. "I didn't have time to tell her yet. Sit down." Zende pulled out a chair for the newcomer.

Diamond extended her hand to Kamilah. "Zende's a good friend. I come in peace."

The wait staff returned and stood off to the side, waiting until Diamond ordered a spinach salad and hot tea with honey. She refused an alcoholic beverage. "I'm still on the clock for a few more hours."

"Diamond is the best investigator in Hollywood." Zende turned his attention back to Kamilah. "With a little gossip, access to credit cards and personal information, her team can pull together a full report on anybody."

Kamilah sipped her Pinot Noir and leaned into Zende, unconsciously seeking his comfort.

Another, younger waiter placed their salads in front of them.

Diamond took off her glasses and rubbed her face. She wiped smudges off her glasses with the snowy linen, then picked up the threads of the story, "I sent an operative to Brown University. She checked university records and found several people who remembered Dr. Sherman's time on campus."

Diamond opened her Mac and displayed a set of incriminating photos starring a younger Annorah. Diamond looked at Kamilah. "While at Brown, Dr. Sherman dated several women. All of them were pursuing high profile careers and kept their sexual lives below the radar. Annorah engaged in short-term liaisons and did nothing obvious to call attention to herself or the other women. However, we were able to get these compromising photos from a jilted lover."

"I told you Diamond was the best." Zende beamed at Kamilah. He trailed a slow finger up Milah's arm until she shivered. "What else did you uncover, Diamond?"

"Following her divorce, Dr. Sherman spent four months at the Betty Ford Center affiliate in Chicago."

"I didn't know Bette Ford operated other than in Cali." Zende cocked his head.

"The beauty of the Chicago facility is it allows clients to transition back to work and maintain out-patient status. Something she wouldn't have been able to do if she'd gone to California." Diamond continued in her professional voice.

"Noori must've paid a high price for anonymity," Kamilah declared. She scooted her chair forward, disentangling Zende's hand to stare at the evidence on the screen.

Diamond sniggered. "The records were easily hacked. She checked in under her given name. Annorah' s been drinking since she was thirteen and has dabbled in hard drugs. When she left Betty Ford, Dr. Sherman was a recovering high-functioning alcoholic experiencing emotional and internal conflicts, including feelings of shame, remorse, loneliness, and hopelessness. She had no real work experience. She couldn't pass a background check for any reputable research institute dealing with behavioral or sexuality issues. However, she landed a senior research position at The International Truth Institute."

"She got the job because of her father's role in the company," Zende asserted.

Diamond nodded. "My staff pulled all the articles she's authored. She intersperses fact with fiction and uses an expensive university education to confuse and terrorize people." Zende had shared the blogs and articles Noori sent to Reese. "Some of the ones she sent to Reese were personal. They don't show up anywhere else in her writings. There's a real pattern in them."

Kamilah looked shocked.

Initially, Zende had wanted to shield her from most of the ugliness, hoping they would convince Noori to cut her losses once he and Reese showed her how vulnerable she really was. However, Reese said Noori never accepted anything other than her own version of reality.

"Her father's also her agent. Some of his contacts came up with new television and university speaking opportunities if she could pull off a substantiated exposé on high-profile African American preachers. She's been collecting background information and dirt on several of these men for over a year now. And you both know she could write a book about Reese."

"Maybe she'll stop this vendetta if she knows Reese has the goods on her." Kamilah squeezed her eyes and rubbed her fists across them.

"Noori's invested too much in the game. She won't believe any report from Diamond or even Saint Peter opening up his books." Zende spelled it out for Kamilah.

"I'm here to fill you in because you were anxious for an update with what we've uncovered so far. We fact-check as much as possible." Diamond reassured them. "Give me another couple of days to have a clean report prepared. When you lay the evidence in front of her backers, you want it to be both compelling and factual."

The following morning, Zende was in the living room, waiting for Kamilah to join him. Due to the excruciating pain in her leg, they hailed a Lyft for the return trip to the W. Kamilah's leg spasms kept her awake most of the night.

Zende heard a restless Reese leave the penthouse suite earlier. With the private investigator's report, surely Noori would favor an out-of-court settlement to preserve her career. Reese could resign from The Cathedral with the least amount of damage. Now he was back and apparently worse for having gone outside.

"Damn, man, I told you to be careful." Reese threw the tabloid newspaper on the dining table set up in the suite's living room.

Zende picked up the gossip rag and perused it.

132

Who's the mystery woman? Zende Lightbourn was spotted going into a fancy Chicago restaurant last night, accompanied by an unknown woman. Lightbourn had his arm wrapped tightly around the woman, and she wore a fur hat obscuring her face. Keeping out of the public eye since leaving Los Angeles, the "recovering" Lightbourn is putting his sabbatical to good use. When we reached out to his manager, Walter Johnson told us "Zende's healing and hoping to be back in the studio soon." We'll be keeping a sharp eye out for other sightings.

Zende scrunched up his eyes, and his hands pinched the bridge of his nose. "It was a dinner date, man. The hawk was treacherous, and there was ice coating the sidewalks. I was holding on to Milah to keep her from slipping or doing further injury to her leg."

"How noble." Reese sneered as he helped himself to pomegranate juice. "Tell that to the paparazzi and the gossip columns."

"What are you getting so worked up for? No one knows." He looked at the paper one more time before tossing it to the side.

"I'll bet one person can figure it out." Reese's mouth twitched. He finished his juice. He set the glass down before it shattered.

Zende's uncomfortable gaze fell. "If you'd seen Kamilah's eyes sparkling last night, it was worth this mention in the paper. As my mother used to say to my father when the children were seated at the table: Sugar! Honey! Ice! Tea!" He acknowledged his friend's conflicted emotions. "How did it go last night?"

Reese balled up his fists and boxed with an imaginary opponent while relaying the outcome of the meeting. "Noori is a cornered rabid animal whose foot is in the trap. She must either lose the foot or kill herself. Either way, she's going to come out swinging."

"What's your defense?" Zende pressed him. Reese hadn't yet met the barracuda Zende had dinner with recently. He had no knowledge of her past sexual history with women. Reese better have all the ammunition lined up at the starting gate. The preacher couldn't imagine how her personal vendetta had morphed into a professional focus on him.

"The truth."

Zende scoffed, "Who's going to believe you, 'David,' versus Noori, 'Goliath'?"

"The crowds underestimated David. A weakling. Young. No armor. No sword. Five rocks and a slingshot. I don't have five rocks. I only have one." Reese's swag was evident as his voice fell into the rhythm of a Baptist preacher.

"Will it be enough?" Zende's voice proclaimed his skepticism. He'd deflate Reese's ego now rather than let him believe intellectual "truth" was gonna work for him. This was the point he kept pressing with Milah about Reese's "Peter Pan" tendencies.

"Yes. My God is able."

"My private investigator shared some intel you might want to hear. Sit down and listen."

Reese sat. What he heard left him speechless and for once, hopeful. Until his phone rang.

Reese listened to Grace's voice on the other end telling him "Genesis is pretty banged up. He raped her. We're still in the emergency room, waiting for them to finish up the exam."

"We're leaving now." He stared at Zende. "Genesis is in the hospital. She was sexually assaulted last night."

CHAPTER TWENTY-FOUR: KAMILAH

KAMILAH, MISTY, AND MISTY'S girlfriend formed a circle around Genesis, praying for her physical and emotional healing. Due to the sensitivity of the matter, the attending doctor asked Reese to remain in the waiting room. Genesis looked like what she was: a scared young girl with a black eye, a bump on her forehead and wearing a cornflower blue cotton hospital gown. Marks ringed her neck, bruises visible from her chest to her knees, and a couple of broken nails. Although the out-of-control teen provided the venue for smoking and drinking, allowed her girlfriend to be sexually assaulted and didn't helped her in the aftermath and gave the young man mixed signals, she didn't deserve to be raped.

Misty opened the door to admit a uniformed female police officer with permanent frown lines. The woman's eyes were kind. "My name is Officer Grady. I'm here to interview Genesis Hardeman."

"I'm her mother." Misty pointed to the bed.

The seasoned officer, trained to deal with rape and assault victims, pulled up a chair and sat next to Genesis. She spoke calmly and with a sense of having been in this situation before. "The rape kit came back with semen in your cervix. When the officers picked Calvin up, they confiscated his clothing. Seems like he didn't take a shower after leaving your place. There was a match for the semen in his underwear and on his jeans. He's in police custody now and will remain there until a hearing before a judge."

"I hope he gets raped in jail...the punk!" Misty interrupted the officer.

Kamilah placed a hand on Misty's tense arm. Misty shut up and rolled her eyes to the ceiling.

The officer twisted her mouth and turned her cold blue eyes directly toward Misty. "His family lawyered up. The lawyer's taken witness statements from some of your daughter's friends." The officer consulted her notebook and read the names of girls who attended the various after-school parties Genesis hosted while Misty was working or out socializing with friends.

"He was too damn old for you. He's twenty years old and lives with his mama. He flunked outta college. He ain't about shit." Misty screeched and flung out a hand toward Genesis.

The officer made a note of Misty's comments.

"Now he gonna say you instigated yo own rape." Angry tears spurted from the mother's eyes, and she kept spilling her anger.

Grace sat down beside Misty and grabbed hold of her hands.

Genesis shook her head negatively and pointed the finger at Misty. "You was gonna be out late. I was grounded so I invited him over."

"Was Friday night the first time you invited him over for sex?" The officer made another note as she continued the interview.

Stupid question, lady. This little girl been playing her momma forever. You are the only one in this room who doesn't know her history.

"No... but it was the first time he came over when nobody else was there." The girl's trembling fingers pleated the bed sheet as tears slid down her face. "Sometimes we'd leave the others in the living room, go into my bedroom and have

136

oral sex. I'd do him, and he'd do me." She swiped the tears from her eyes and avoided her mother mean-mugging her. "Calvin wanted to be the one to break me in."

Kamilah hid her face behind her hand, scrunched her eyes, and then reached for a wad of tissues. This was eerily reminiscent of the night Genesis snuck into their apartment. Genesis' desire to grow up too fast. To conceive a baby who would love her. Only now, fright tempered the harsh words the girl uttered. *Please, God. Be a fence around this rebellious child who has crossed a line that can't be uncrossed. The ramifications are going to be a game-changer for her.*

"Last night, we were in my bedroom… after oral, Calvin told me if I was gonna be his woman, I needed to get wit the program…right now." Her body shifted in the bed, and she cried out in pain.

The machines recording her vitals spiked, alerting the women in the room to both the girl's psychic and physical pain. When Genesis settled down, she took up her recitation. "We smoked some weed, and I was feeling him. I told him he had to use a raincoat. He ignored me and stripped down to his shorts." Genesis peered at the officer from her downcast eyes. "I'm not havin some random baby. Calvin insisted he liked it raw and since I was a virgin, I couldn't get pregnant."

Misty got up and moved to the window. She banged her head against the window. Kamilah and Misty's friend comforted her. Listening to her child recount how she set up the events of last night had to remind her of the times she'd schemed with Frank to deceive his wife.

"He ripped off my panties and refused to put on a condom." Genesis cried uncontrollably, reliving the trauma. "I kept sayin no…no glove…no love. He got mad, straddled me and started pushing me down on my back."

"We have pictures from the ER showing the bruises on your body." The officer confirmed her statement. "Did you put any marks on him?"

137

"I kicked him and scratched his face, I think. I was trying to buck him off, to make him stop. He laughed and said it was too late...I already told him he could do it."

Forget purity classes. Forget abstinence. You play with a man, lead him on and then say no. He's no longer thinking. Rape is never justified. Somebody better teach this girl some self-defense tactics and critical thinking skills. She needs counseling to set higher standards for herself.

The officer's next words corroborated what Genesis said. "The results of the examination showed bruising on your neck, upper torso, lower body and what looks like handprints on your inner thighs. There's vaginal tearing, and you're going to be sore for a while. Was this your first time?"

The teen nodded, wiping her hand across her nose. Genesis knew nothing about sex. Unfortunately, she'd always remember her sexual initiation at the hands of a boy who violated her trust and took what she denied him. The bravado was finally wearing off. She was acknowledging she'd been dishonored by someone who claimed to be her boyfriend.

"Did he hold your legs open during sex?" the officer asked.

"Yes. ...it felt like burning and tearing...he wouldn't stop. I pounded him, and he kept doing it until he was finished. There was blood on the sheets and on my legs. Calvin said we'd do it again when he caught his breath."

"What did you do?"

"Ran into the bathroom and locked the door. I finally heard the backdoor slam. I was still in the bathroom when Misty came home." She turned her nose up at her mother's name as though the ramifications of her questionable judgment were Misty's fault.

"Please sit down, Ms. Hardeman." The officer motioned for Misty to sit near her.

Misty sat.

"Do you have an attorney?"

Misty shook her head.

"The department's worked previously with the attorney Calvin's family hired. He's a fierce advocate for young men like Calvin. The legal system is going to put Genesis on trial. When this is over, there are going to be two convictions."

"Huh." Misty threw up her hands and looked to Kamilah.

Kamilah translated for her. "The law is specific. A girl under seventeen cannot consent to sex... even when she's willing. The lawyer, however, is going to present the witness statements to the judge and call several witnesses to corroborate his client's version of the facts."

"I don't understand." Misty clearly watched too much *Law and Order SUV*. In the real world, a high-profile lawyer would crucify Genesis. The girl's attitude and refusal to accept any responsibility would cast doubt on her testimony. Her previous shameless acts would be entered into the record. The only saving grace was Misty brought her to the Emergency Room instead of giving her a shower and putting her to bed.

"He's trying to plead his client down to the lowest level...a misdemeanor with the least amount of jail time," the officer said bluntly,

"You've seen her...the bruises. She said no," Misty yelped.

"Yes. And one of Genesis' friends said she recently tried to seduce a married man."

Kamilah's heart dropped. This nightmare never ended.

"What does that have to do with anything? He raped her."

"I hate to say it, but it's going to depend on the judge and the jury. A lot of judges subscribe to the boys will be boys notion. The same judges believe any girl over eight years of age is a slut waiting to happen."

"What should I do?"

"Hire the best attorney you can afford and dig up some better character witnesses."

CHAPTER TWENTY-FIVE:
NOORI

O N THE MORNING OF the Ethics inquest against Dr. Annorah Sherman, the eight committee members assembled at the conference table in the chairman's suite of offices. The chairman sat at the center of the table, conferring with the audiovisual team members. Microphones were placed in front of the participants and checked for sound quality. The hearing was being videoed and audiotaped. No visitors were allowed in the chambers.

Luna Erickson entered the room in her professional attire: a navy-blue pantsuit and cream-colored man-tailored shirt. She carried a thick case file with multiple colored tags, probably intended to cite every APA case of the past century. She gave Annorah a terse nod.

Erickson's sidekick, Dr. Warren, tsked at Annorah like a grandmother. Dr. Warren wore a stunning high-low red, gold, and brown African print dress in a shirt style with a full circle bottom, long sleeves, buttons, and pockets. Her elegant dress, Bantu knots and diminutive size disguised a lioness in her protectiveness of the university and the psychology profession.

These two women needed to sit down. The permissive era they represented had passed. The academy required vibrant new scholars to affirm the truth of human behavior as decreed by the Bible.

Reese Thompkins sat at another table with the assistant who was transcribing the hearing. Noori stared at Reese, scrutinizing his elegantly dressed self. Her stomach twisted into a knot. He wore a European cut charcoal gray slimline suit with a dark gray collarless shirt. His shoes were designed by Santoni. She rolled her eyes and bit the inside of her mouth. She'd spent years tracking his ministry and music career. Other than seeing him preaching at The Cathedral, this was the closest she'd been to him since she ended their affair.

The International Truth Institute hired Graham Hurd to represent Dr. Annorah Sherman in this witch hunt. She and her attorney sat at a table facing the committee members. She'd dazzled The Institute Board with bull shit. The governing body had no idea of the substance of the investigations and assumed it was a vendetta against her by a former professor.

Attorney Hurd stood and preempted the chair's opening remarks. "Mr. Chairman, while this is highly irregular, my client wishes to make a statement. We believe that once you hear from Dr. Sherman, this kangaroo court can be disbanded without any harm coming to Mr. Thompkins for filing these false charges."

Noori stared at Reese to ensure he saw the contempt in her eyes and on her face.

Reese neither acknowledged her nor flinched.

"Mr. Hurd…as legal adviser, you know the process. The committee members are the ones asking the questions. Sit down." The chairman's eyes were flat and deadly …like a cobra's before it strikes.

Noori chose not to play by their rules. She stood up. Dressed carefully for this circus, her tailored fuchsia suit, short skirt, tightly fitted jacket, perfect new hairstyle and make-up screamed 'I'm the star here'.

"Councilor, does your client have a hearing problem?" The chairman banged his gavel. "Dr. Sherman will have an opportunity to rebut the charges when we get to the testimony part of the agenda. Tell your client to sit down so that we might proceed."

"This sham inquiry is interfering with the delicate nature of Dr. Sherman's ongoing research." The legal representative put his hand on her arm.

Noori forced herself to chill.

Because Dr. Erickson doesn't agree with Dr. Sherman's research methodology doesn't make Dr. Sherman wrong or out of bounds." Noori's legal adviser tossed out one more grenade just as they'd practiced.

"Dr. Erickson did not file the charges. The university did." The chairman admonished the lawyer. "This is not a research inquiry, Mr. Hurd. This is an ethics inquiry."

Noori's blood pumped fast and furiously through her veins. Her mouth twisted and she bit her bottom lip. The university was taking this drama more seriously than she predicted during her advisors' strategy session.

"Dr. Sherman was conducting her personal style of research." The legal advice-giver defended his client. "It's possible Mr. Thompkins misunderstood her kindness and confused it with personal interest."

"Sex with a patient is not research," the chairman growled. "For the last time, sit down, or we'll conclude these tactics are designed to keep your client from answering our questions."

The legal advisor continued reading from his notes and addressed the chair. "Were there witnesses to this sexual liaison? My client denies any inappropriate sexual behavior with Mr. Thompkins."

"Then she'll have no problem facing her accuser." The chairman scowled.

Dr. Sherman's legal advisor's face reddened. "He said, she said. This hearing is absurd. A pillar of the community versus a deluded, rejected transsexual." He gripped his pen. He slashed words on his notepad.

The chairman banged the gavel on the hardwood table. "Mr. Hurd, you are misconstruing the scope and seriousness of this inquiry."

"The university is making a mistake by dragging Dr. Sherman through this travesty of an investigation. We'll take legal action against the university and this committee to ensure no adverse reaction for my client."

"Mr. Hurd, is there a question in there somewhere or an implied threat?"

The lawyer replied, "No."

"Shut up and sit down." The chairman brought the gavel down.

Chairman Hallstrom laid out the facts of the case as a stenographer recorded the proceedings.

Noori felt the committee members' eyes on her, judging her, and probably hoping she would capitulate. Once the chairman completed his opening statement, she interrupted. "Nobody pays any attention to APA."

"Dr. Sherman, did you engage in a sexual relationship with Reese Thompkins while he was a patient of Dr. Erickson's?" The chairman asked pointedly.

"What's wrong?" She waved him off, deflecting the question.

"Please answer the question." the chairman persisted.

This kangaroo court had gotten beyond her control. Reese was telling the world they had sex before the transition. "The relationship, if you want to call it that, happened over six years ago."

"Is your answer yes?"

"I have more to do than listen to these half-truths and speculation by academics who've already made up their minds to discredit anyone who doesn't 'get with their program.'" Her fingers crooked over the words *get with their program.*

The chairman rapped his gavel on the table. "Dr. Sherman, do you understand the consequences of this matter and the potential-crippling blow to your career?" He stared at Noori.

Her lips tightened; her shoulders were pulled up to her ears by thin wires. "The truth needs to be told about these disgusting freaks." Noori dropped her eyes, unable to stand the criticism and fury in her former employer's eyes.

After naming the men involved, the chairman reiterated. "Did you exploit these three men named in the complaint and use their personal information to write articles promoting your views."

Noori sucked in a deep breath. "Who are these degenerates you think I harmed?" She needed a stiff drink. *No, you need sober eyes. Handle yo bizness.*

"One of the three people you harmed was living in a halfway house in a supportive living environment." The chairman pulled up another case file. "His roommate met you and witnessed the interactions. He threatened to blow the whistle on the patient about the precise nature of the sexual relationship. The patient cut off contact with you."

"I gave the shim a ride home. It was meant to be helpful. His roommate was a recovering drunk. He must have misunderstood what he saw."

"Dr. Sherman, this hearing is a matter of public record. You are not helping your cause with the use of defamatory language. You admit to driving the man home from a bar around 11:00 p.m. You disclosed drinking with a client. You acknowledge leaving lipstick on his shirt collar. Was this the regular time and place where you conducted your social histories?"

Noori rolled her eyes and said nothing. The tension in the room was as thick as smoke belching from the Gary, Indiana steel mills.

"You and another patient went to the movies on several occasions." The chairman read from a third case file. "He became suspicious when you insisted on meeting in a dimly lit bar. There was no pretense of work related to those meetings because you had already completed the social history."

"Nothing happened. The faker wanted me to hear his whole life story."

"The social history was the designated tool for getting his life story." Sarcasm and a bit of street thug were attached to each of the chairman's clipped words. "He tested your fake interest in him. The man invited you to be his date for a Sunday dinner with his family."

"I have dinner with my family every Sunday. We attend church services together, first." Whew! Noori didn't have to fabricate an excuse for this one. She grinned. *Go. Check it out.*

"Your unwillingness to meet his family, however, was a deal breaker. He broke off contact with you."

Some loose talk. Noori could manage that.

"We have pictures, too." The chairman's off-handed remark caused her smile to disappear for good. Noori could barely remember the other two shims now. She was drinking and whoring around while daddy-dumbest was pushing Dolton down her throat.

"Wait up! I have a right to see these pictures if they exist. Anything can be photoshopped," the legal advisor objected.

"Mr. Hurd, if you or your client had bothered to come to the prearranged conference, you would have received the entire evidentiary file."

"Dr. Sherman." The chair turned his attention back to her. "The committee will ask APA to consider revoking your license to practice and suing The International Truth Institute for money damages. The negative publicity will affect your writing and speaking career. Who will come out to hear a woman who engages in the same behavior she stigmatizes?"

Noori shifted her gaze from the committee chairman to Reese. "Thompkins will be more humiliated when the world learns Pastor Reese is a woman. I can write the story my damn self." She turned a malicious stare at him, warning "A tranny. She'll be the laughingstock of the Christian world."

Reese looked her in the eye, unblinking and emotionless.

Hateful, evil words spewed from her mouth. "This isn't over, Thompkins. I'll see you in hell before I let you and your kind corrupt the kingdom of God."

CHAPTER TWENTY-SIX: REESE

SO MUCH FOR TRYING to defuse this Israeli/Palestinian family feud rationally. Noori wanted a fight, and she was determined to get one. Dr. Annorah Sherman admitted violating APA ethics codes by engaging in a personal friendship with Reese. She denied the sexual relationship. It was a minor infraction not worthy of the fuss.

The committee spent three weeks in deliberations following the hearing. There were numerous meetings between the attorneys on both sides, the APA Ethics Oversight Committee, the university hierarchy, public relations firms, state and local political representatives. This unprecedented ethics inquiry rocked the foundation of the university community and the psychiatric community.

Closed door meetings and contingency planning disrupted Drs. Erickson's and Warren's professional lives. The final hearing was being videoed and audiotaped in the event of further litigation. The committee members reassembled at the same conference table. Reese, accompanied by his lawyer, Sybil King, sat at the table on the right, facing the committee. Attorney King was African American, in her fifties, and wicked smart. The legal scholar handled high profile cases before the Illinois State Supreme Court and consulted on matters headed to the US Supreme Court.

Noori, dressed in a bright peacock blue power suit and her high-priced mouthpiece entered the hearing room as though this was a typical presentation of her latest anti-gay rhetoric disguised as research. Her lawyer was subdued today. They acknowledged the committee members and sat at the table across from Reese and his attorney.

After the chairman gaveled the meeting to order, he addressed her calmly, "Dr. Sherman, you preyed on three people we identified. You may have preyed on others who have not come forward."

Noori's wary eyes darted around the table, taking the measure of the members. "The APA will not touch me," she retorted. "Let's get this charade over. The university and this committee will be sued for defamation." Her words were hard as nails, but the voice wobbled. She lacked the confidence she'd displayed three weeks earlier.

"Before we issue our recommendations, Mr. Thompkins has asked to address Dr. Sherman personally." The chairman banged his gavel. "As the injured party, he has the right to let you know the extent of the damage you've caused him."

The legal advisor leaned into Noori's personal space to get her attention. Noori flung out her balled fists, throwing a childish tantrum.

Reese couldn't hear the heated exchange. Her extravagant head and neck gestures screamed she didn't intend to heed the attorney's counsel. The lawyer wrote a word on his pad and pushed it towards her.

Her shoulders sagged. Her red-rimmed eyes shot daggers at the committee chairman. Noori's arrogant voice and chin lifted in response to the chair's request. "Whatever Thompkins says has no standing with me."

"Mr. Thompkins. Proceed." The chairman pointed to him.

Reese stood and walked to the front of the room to face her. "Noori.". He looked directly into her troubled eyes. Hers was the first to drop.

The legal advisor wrote furiously. Noori rearranged her defiant face into a passive, reserved look.

"During the nine months we were involved, were you wearing a mask, laughing at me, and planning to screw me over emotionally as well as physically?" Reese squared his shoulders, endeavoring to keep his voice firm and sure.

Noori refused to meet his eyes.

"You claimed to accept my maleness." Reese was a man standing solidly in his truth. The heat in her eyes would have scorched him had he not prepared and prayed. He couldn't move forward unless he acknowledged his guilt in this so-called relationship. He made eye contact with others in the room, witnessed blank stares, pity, or support on their faces. "I wrote music and poetry for you." The romantic ballads were part of his legacy. Several had generated number one hits for him.

"With my limited funds, I purchased your favorite coffee and Danish, Chicago style pizza, and Thai take-out." He let out a breath, much like Savannah in *Waiting to Exhale*. The worst was behind him. All he had to do was wrap it up and move on to the next phase of his life.

Noori laughed at him, her chest heaving as her composure cracked. He knew the telltale signs. He wouldn't turn around to witness the committee members' pitying looks.

"Sex and admissions of love meant nothing to me. You were easy to play," Noori yelled out, her lip curled and her eyes malevolent. Her lawyer grabbed her arm and motioned for her to be quiet.

"Mr. Hurd, if your client has one more outburst, she will be removed from this hearing." The chairman's words were clipped. "Do you understand me?"

"Yes, sir." The legal advisor spoke to Noori, probably pointing out what was at stake. She tried to stare Reese down to no avail.

"If there was a fraud committed, it was by you." Reese ignored the childish outburst. "I never pretended. I didn't withhold information or emotions from you."

Noori jumped up, striding towards the door. When she reached it, she turned back and screamed at him, "I'd forgotten all about you until you called from Belgrade."

Reese fisted his hands at his sides.

Her lawyer raced to her side, preventing her from leaving the room.

The Ethics Committee members stared at Reese with varying expressions of respect and sadness. The only sound was the stenographer's fingers recording the accused's guilty statements.

"Since the surgery and transition, you've shown me nothing but contempt, hate, and veiled threats." Reese faced his tormentor.

Bitterness and snarkiness rendered Noori's face an ugly mask. The lawyer's firm grip on her left arm kept her immobile.

"An answer to this question will help me close this regrettable episode in my life." Reese stood still until she acknowledged him with a lift of her chin, like a prize fighter sticking his chin out to an unworthy opponent. "Did I tap into feelings you hadn't acknowledged before ... or was I a lab rat, somebody you manipulated for your selfish pleasures?"

"You mistook sex for a relationship." Noori snapped, breaking free of her lawyer, lunging toward him. "You were a poor little sex-starved virgin. You were a pet begging for affection, and I gave it to you. Did you think I'd compromise my future or turn my life upside down for a shim."

Shim was the absolute insult for a transsexual.

"How do you justify the deliberate cruelty, the articles, the stalking..." Reese lifted his eyes to see her clearly for the first time. He wanted her cruel words on the record inorder to be free of her. Forever.

Totally out of control, she screamed, "My first responsibility is what's best for me. My life matters. The aspirations of my parents matter."

The chairman brought the gavel down. "Mr. Hurd, you have ten minutes to calm your client down. This hearing is in recess."

CHAPTER TWENTY-SEVEN: REESE

REESE WALKED OUT OF the conference room to clear his head. He could heal now. With the information Zende gleaned from Diamond's contacts and Noori's words in the hearing room, Reese could put this disaster behind him. He headed for the water fountain and drank deeply of the cold water. When he turned around, the former lovers were face-to-face.

"Yo act in there was pathetic. I never loved you." Noori's shoulders arched and her back was military straight.

"Thanks for your honesty." Reese neither flinched nor retreated. Today was his last encounter with Noori. He'd taken a scalpel to an infected wound, and the ugly poison was draining out of his system. Reese blocked out the murmuring in the background. He needed to go home and wash the stench off.

Ms. King raised her hand in a questioning gesture.

Reese smiled and dipped his head. *No worries.*

Ms. King dug out her phone and tapped a note.

Reese's phone vibrated. He read the text. *Remain calm.*

He hit a smiling emoji and returned the text.

"With your 'story' in there, you ruined my gig." His former lover snapped in a menacing tone. "I bet you slipped some designer date rape drugs in my drinks, put roots on me or had an island conjure woman cast a spell."

Reese's eyes darted around the hallway, assuring himself no one was picking up the vile words coming out of her mouth.

Several of the committee members stationed themselves a way off, casting furtive glances toward the pair. The ombudsman walked toward them but was halted by Noori's attorney who engaged him in a rapid-fire conversation while gesturing toward Dr. Erickson. Noori's attorney blamed Erickson for Reese's actions. *Noori was demon possessed.*

Noori stared off into the recesses of the hallway for a minute, then spoke in a sarcastic tone, "I got attached to you and let it go on too long." She leveled a hostile glare at him. "Years later, I looked up, and you were the new Senior Pastor at The Cathedral. Strutting around like you got swag. I threw up." She swiped her shaky hand across her mouth. "The laugh was on me. I never believed your con could work."

"No deception here." Reese blew out a frustrated breath. He was an idiot for engaging in a conversation after what had transpired in the hearing room.

"Being rewarded with multi-platinum records. Receiving awards with the incestuous wifey by your side." Noori mocked him. "I decided to keep an eye on you." Noori watched him with eyes that could burn flesh. "What you are is an abomination to God. With meticulous documentation and photos of you before the mutilation, I will reveal how the homosexual agenda is seeping into the pulpits of churches."

"What homosexual agenda?" The hairs on Reese's arms stood up.

"It wasn't good enough for you to act like a male with a woman. Nah, you wanted to be a man." Her shrill voice was unhinged.

"Noori, something's twisted in you." Needing a breath of fresh air, Reese maneuvered around her. She reeked of fear and medicinal mouthwash to cover the stench of alcohol oozing from her pores. He pointed to himself. "I am what God intended me to be. He has ordered my steps from the beginning. The whispers and naysayers do not change me." Reese was weary of this conflict and prepared to move on with his life. "What's it going to take to end this?"

WINTER'S LAMENT

"You in a body bag."

CHAPTER TWENTY-EIGHT: REESE

WHEN THE INQUIRY RECONVENED, the chairman spoke from a prepared statement. "By your own admission, Dr. Sherman, you engaged in an inappropriate sexual relationship with Mr. Thompkins and inflicted intentional harm on him." The chairman paused.

"He had the surgery and entered into an incestuous relationship with his sister," Noori interrupted.

"You engaged in cyber-bullying and cyber-stalking. Mr. Thompkins retained the articles and the envelopes you sent to him. He preserved the texts and emails." The chairman stared at her.

Noori's mouth flew open. She hadn't considered the possibility of physical evidence linking her to him. Her wild eyes swiveled to confront Reese.

Seriously, Noori. You thought I'd put my life on the line with nothing to back me up.

"The committee reviewed the videotape of your appearance at The Cathedral."

The committee members' eyes fastened on her face. Noori turned dead eye sockets toward Reese, her mouth opening, and closing.

"We compared the actual sermon to the blog you posted." The chairman passed copies of the numerous pieces of evidence to Noori's attorney. "Mr. Thompkins asked you, in writing, to take the inflammatory document down."

"It's my intellectual property. I could have outed him on the spot," She spat.

"That was your end game?" The chairman asked as he jotted a note on his tablet.

"Hell yes. This pathetic s.o.b. passes himself off as a married man. Bullshit lies. When I get through with him, he will be on the streets: broke, humiliated and living with other scum."

The committee chair banged his gavel. "Dr. Sherman, you are a disgrace to the profession."

"There's no such a thing as transgendered. I wanted to meet the freaks who are so messed up they take drugs and butcher their bodies," Noori clapped back

Dr. Erickson and Dr. Warren gave her disapproving looks but held their tongues.

"These freaks need hospitalization. The profession needs to be revising shock treatments and lobotomies instead of coddling them and telling them they're okay," She screeched, "The Bible says, man and woman. Not Crossdressers! Not Transvestites! Not Transgendered!"

"What does it say about dedicating years to study a behavioral arena where you didn't respect the work or the people who engage in it," Dr. Warren countered.

"There's nothing you can tell me. The only truth comes from the Bible." Noori pulled her lips back in a snarl. "My dad spent his life fighting the church to hold the line on this one issue. I told my daddy... pay for my degree. I'll become an instrument for the destruction of the homosexual agenda. I'll infiltrate it. Get up close and personal."

Based on photos and interviews Zende's PI conducted, Noori was lying. She didn't care about the truth.

Zeline Warren got up from her seat at the committee table, walked over and sat down next to Noori, clasping her hands, "Annorah, you can't have gone through the academic process and still parrot this uneducated bullshit. Stop rationalizing your behavior by minimizing Reese Thompkins' life."

Wrenching her hands away, Noori stood up and paced the room. "She must be stopped. Her name is Rielle. She was born Rielle Thompkins... a girl." She screamed the words. "I rebuke the demons! I won't let Satan have the victory!"

Dr. Warren voice cut through Noori's self-absorbed rant. "You're not the authority on Reese Thompkins' sexuality or sexual identity. He was vulnerable, searching, seeking friendship and love. You violated his trust to satisfy your sexual desires." Dr. Warren's eyes darted back and forth. "You degraded him in ways far crueler and dehumanizing than any bigot who beat him down out of their ignorance and homophobia."

"Rielle was wrong. She destroyed her body, her temple God created to perpetrate this fraud." Noori refused to consider the ethical violations.

If I can face this, I can deal with anything.

"Regardless of who lied and agreed to this farce," Noori pointed a shaky finger at Dr. Erickson, "it sickens me. I was attracted to Rielle Thompkins who had breasts, a flat stomach, and a vagina. I was attracted to her body. I was confused and the situation got out of hand."

The committee chair intervened. "Dr. Sherman, you are minimizing your continuing lapses in judgment. You're casting yourself as the victim here."

Noori pleaded, "Homosexuality is a choice. It is an unacceptable lifestyle. God's way is the only way."

"Sit down, Annorah." Luna Erickson barked like a drill sergeant. "You're suffering from an emotional breakdown because of your closeted lesbianism. In your confusion, homophobia, and religious doctrine, you've combined multiple arguments. You've corrupted a hundred years of work to eradicate misunderstandings about sexual orientation and sexual identity as two separate and distinct phenomena."

Noori's eyes rolled around in her head. Her make-up streaked and ran down her cheeks. Her body slumped over. "You wouldn't have hired me if I disagreed with you."

Luna Erickson pounded on the table. "There's no litmus test in psychology other than scholarly research and the ability to defend your positions."

The other members looked at Noori with disapproving eyes.

"You pretended to believe in my research when you could've gone to a university where the staff was aligned with your religious views."

Noori's eyes flashed anger and hostility.

"You're still plotting to do this pseudo exposé on a person you claimed to care about." Dr. Erickson spat out.

Noori shrugged. "It is what it is. It was a disgusting episode frowned on by my church and my family. I went back to God. I had to uncross the line because I won't be rejected by my family." Having told so many lies, Noori didn't know the truth anymore.

"We're done here." The chairman refocused the committee on the APA ethics charges and their data collection. "It's time to move on and submit the committee's recommendations."

Annorah sat motionless until the chairman finished his remarks and gaveled the meeting to an end.

Reese wanted to go home and sort this out with Kamilah. While he could forgive, Noori still posed a threat to his ministry. His job was to protect the congregation.

CHAPTER TWENTY-NINE:
KAMILAH

RESTLESS IN SPIRIT AND body, Kamilah dozed as she and Zende waited for Reese in the living room of their quarters. The duo's future was bound up in the outcome of the hearing. Since their return from the thwarted trip to Chicago, Kamilah had begun preparations for their inevitable exit. She'd donated most of her winter clothing to regional shelters and women's centers. She'd separated her kitchen utensil purchases from those belonging to the Winston House and donated them to an organization helping families rebuild after the tornado. Finally, she'd moved all her books and videos to the youth ministry department where the kids could help themselves to whatever they wanted.

Reese texted her at the end of the hearing. He was upset and rambling. Ready to escape for a spiritual retreat after resigning his position at The Cathedral. He hadn't wanted it to end like this, but the choice was no longer his. Noori would wreak devastation worse than last fall's tornado. He should have been home by now.

Zende refused to return to his campus living space until Reese relayed the hearing outcome. If the results were as terrible as they imagined, the paparazzi would pounce on Zende, searching for dirt and scandal. While Zende didn't care, his family's conservative political life would be affected. Moreover, he wanted nothing to interfere with his plans to marry Kamilah as soon as this was over.

Kamilah's phone beeped, and she answered it. She automatically checked the time. 10:33 p.m.

"Ma'am… Ms. Thompkins, this is the Pontiac Sheriff's department."

"Yes …what's going on?" Her heart seized as she took in several quick breaths. "Reese?"

"Ms. Thompkins, your husband's been in a car accident." The practiced, polite voice held a trace of a southern twang.

"No." She stood up on unsteady legs, hot tears pricking at the back of her eyelids. Her throat clenched, holding back a scream. Zende stepped up behind her, cradling her back against his front. She leaned into him, absorbing his strength. She hit the speaker button on the phone.

"Listen, ma'am … he's alive … he's pretty banged up. His vehicle was totaled." The disembodied voice was matter of fact. "The ambulance is transporting him to the OSF Saint James—John Albrecht Medical Center in Pontiac." The officer may as well have been reading from a script.

"What happened?" Reese knew the poor quality of the roads and drove a SUV designed for heavy duty driving. He'd been driving these highways for years either going to doctors' appointments or touring with regional musicians. Did Noori follow him? Put a hit on him? Did that witch harm him?

"Mr. Thompkins' Land Rover was heading south on Interstate 55 when he was hit head-on just outside Pontiac. The officer on the scene took witness statements. The driver of the car that struck him hit a patch of black ice, skidded and lost control of his vehicle. The vehicle was headed in the wrong direction when it slid across the lane and rammed into the front of the Land Rover on the driver's side."

"How badly is he hurt?" Alive was no comfort if he were severely injured or less than the vital man he'd always been.

"Mr. Thompkins got the worst of it. The car traveling behind the Land Rover slammed on its brakes and crashed into the back of Mr. Thompkins car." The sheriff reported. "We won't know the extent of his injuries until the emergency room personnel examine him."

"Is he conscious?" Her heart was thudding, her hands shaking, barely keeping it together as scenes flashed behind her eyelids of Reese severely injured and alone on a dark, icy highway.

"In and out. The airbags deployed. Probably saved his life."

"I'm on my way." Kamilah turned, and Zende nodded.

The sheriff gave her the address and hung up. Zende's sinewy arms held her until the shaking stopped. "Let's go."

As Zende navigated the icy roads to Pontiac, Kamilah prayed for God to hold Reese in His arms until she could reach him. Singing. Crying. Worrying about the extent of new injuries to his body after the previous surgeries.

The fifty-mile drive took two hours with slowing down to accommodate the highway covered in black ice. They rushed to the trauma center where two white police officers met them. "Are you Mrs. Thompkins?" The older, senior officer approached them as they entered the door and addressed them.

"I'm Kamilah Thompkins."

"The doctor will see you immediately." The middle-aged officer escorted them down a hall and into a private family room. Less than a minute later, the door opened to admit a young ER doctor with curly brown hair pulled up in a messy ponytail, kind topaz eyes, wearing scrubs and holding a clipboard in his hand. "Mrs. Thompkins, I'm Dr. Overton, Emergency Room Physician. Please, sit down." He gestured toward a small rectangular table with four chairs.

Zende pulled out a chair for her and stood behind her like a centurion. The ER doctor sat across from her.

"Is Reese alive?" Kamilah had difficulty voicing her greatest fear.

The ER doctor nodded. "Mr. Thompkins suffered extensive injuries to his upper body, his back and his legs from the impact and deployment of the airbags. He's got cuts and bruises to his face and hands…" Overton's voice was shaky, tenuous. "However, we've got bigger obstacles than saving his life."

Kamilah observed his hands, his nervous mannerisms, and his downcast features. His inability to look her in the eyes revealed the truth. *Here we go again!* When would trans people in general and Reese ever get a fair shake? *God be a fence around Reese.*

"We're performing necessary procedures to stabilize Mr. Thompkins." The ER doctor reached for her hand and held it reassuringly. "We are dealing with a complicated situation here. Small town. Small minds." The emergency room doctor leaned forward in his chair, holding on to her hands and scrutinizing her. "We plan to airlift Mr. Thompkins immediately to White Oaks, a private hospital outside Bolingbrook, IL."

"Are you discriminating against him because he's transgendered?" Kamilah snatched her hand away, fury spreading through her body.

The ER doctor twisted his wedding band as his eyes skittered from Kamilah to Zende, "Yes and no. The health care system's rules and policy would cost me my job for even having this conversation with you." He looked at her with a combination of sympathy and fear.

Zende whispered in her ear. "Hear him out."

The ER doctor rubbed his tired eyes and whooshed out a low breath. "I'm calling attention to our deficits in policy and practice, not to Mr. Thompkins. All the staff here don't operate on the same level of spirit or decency concerning patients' diagnoses or spreading gossip and rumors."

"Speak plainly, doctor." Zende interrupted. "We don't have time to waste on drama. Our only concern is getting Reese the best care."

The physician nodded. "I'm trying to avoid a media circus. I'm a fan of his music. His face is a mess... so far no one else has made the connection."

Zende's stare was malevolent.

"You can bring me up on charges, or you can hear me out. Mr. Thompkins is not going to die. St. James is not the place for him to be treated at or to recover in. We're a small-town hospital. We don't have the specialists who can deal with the multiple levels of the trauma he's experiencing. He's going to need extensive medical treatment for the next couple of months and then ongoing rehab and therapy."

Kamilah's heart sank to the scrubbed and disinfected floor. Most hospitals and their staff didn't bother to learn about sexual reassignment surgery or its implications for ongoing health care. Tears flooded her eyes and fell on the table. The discrimination, ignorance, and intolerance never ended. She focused on the doctor's explanation.

"I want you to decode the message I can't utter in this facility. There's a chopper ready to lift off as soon as you give them the okay. He'll be at White Oaks quickly ... The clinic's interdisciplinary medical team is standing by, ready to do what's required for him. I called ahead and briefed them on Mr. Thompkins status."

"Thank you." She clasped the doctor's hand, accepting this was another step along the path they'd been traveling forever.

Father, I'm leaning and depending on you. No other help I know.

"We were virtually a ghost town when he came in. I was the attending emergency room physician tonight." The doctor raised his eyes to the ceiling. "We're a close-knit group here. Some staff wouldn't be able to keep their mouths shut."

"How soon can we leave?" Zende probed.

"Sign these papers." The doctor pushed the clipboard towards her and handed her a pen. "They'll have him in surgery in less than an hour."

She signed the papers and pushed the clipboard back to him. "Thank you, Dr. Overton. Reese and I appreciate what you did for him tonight."

Kamilah punched in Deacon Slay's number. His sleepy voice answered. "Is something wrong?"

"Reese was in a car accident while driving back from Chicago tonight," Kamilah whooshed out a quivering breath.

"I worry about that boy ripping and running up and down the highway. How badly is he hurt?"

"Deacon Slay, he's pretty banged up and can't have visitors right now. As soon as he's stable, he'll want to talk to you and Rev. Thornton personally." Kamilah lied through her teeth. She had no clue what the doctors were doing or how long it was going to take. She hung onto the words *not life-threatening*.

"What do you need?" The elder always extended graciousness and hospitality.

"We need you to take care of The Cathedral and the campaign. It's a critical time to wrap up the outside donors."

"We can handle it. I'm sorry the deacon board is split over this and haven't done much except grumble."

Kamilah thanked God for Deacon Slay. "I can relay questions and information to Reese." One more lie wouldn't hurt. "If the prospects require a personal touch, I'll handle it.

"When can he have visitors or calls?"

"I'll let you know." She rushed him off the phone; she'd surpassed her quotient of lies.

CHAPTER THIRTY:
KAMILAH

IN TODAY'S OVERSATURATED media environment
where scandal, gossip, and innuendo substituted for facts,
White Oaks was an oasis for reclusive persons and
celebrities desiring anonymity during treatment without media
attention or people willing to sell their secrets. White Oaks was
a fifty-bed state-of-the-art private hospital and rehabilitation
facility tucked away from view in a stand of oak trees. The
exclusive facility boasted high-tech surgeries, physical and
occupational therapy, and mental health counseling. Individual
family suites consisted of a fully equipped hospital room for
the patient, as well as one or two bedrooms and a sitting room
for family members. There were skylights in the bedrooms and
floor to ceiling windows to allow patients and families to view
the pastoral setting of the hospital grounds. Zende had the
forethought to ask for the two-bedroom suite when they were
filling out admission forms and providing payment
information.

Soothing music poured from the surround system instead
of calls for doctors. Specialized physicians, nursing staff and
other allied specialists attended to their patients' daily needs.
The chef, with the assistance of nutritionists, prepared specific
diets for the people under their care. The housekeeping staff
wore hospitality uniforms instead of the scrubs seen in
hospitals. In addition to their professional skills, all team

members were screened for integrity, discretion, and signed confidentiality agreements.

Reese Thompkins was a patient rather than a famous musician, pastor or trans man. Early the next afternoon, a heavily sedated Reese with an NG tube taped to his nose, drifted in and out of consciousness. Because of the massive doses of narcotics, he was not able to do more than open his eyes and groan in distress. He was barely coherent. The on-duty nurse monitored the pain meds and pushed the morphine drip every hour.

"Ms. Thompkins, how did he make it through the morning?" The general surgeon entered the room still wearing the green scrubs from last night.

Kamilah unfolded her exhausted body from the reclining lounger she'd been nodding in. She threw aside the pillow and blanket the nurse brought in when she discovered the woman curled in the fetal position in the cold room around 4:00 a.m. The smooth jazz music pouring from the surround system finally lulled her to sleep. An hour ago, she'd sent Zende out to find a Big Box store where he could pick up a couple of pairs of sweatsuits and toiletries. Neither one thought to pack a bag last night.

"It's been horrible. I can't stop seeing Reese like that." Both his eyes were blackened, his left leg bruised with a massive gash from the impact. The dark bruises on his face gave him the look of a demented raccoon who'd lost the fight over a garbage can. His harsh breathing alarmed her. "I can only imagine the horrors I wasn't privy to."

"Mr. Thompkins' case is complicated, and treatment is going to be convoluted at times, complex and problematic." The surgeon had deep lines around his mouth and bags under his bruised eyes. "We've assembled an extensive team. We're bringing in several specialists to consult and to work through the challenges." The doctor scrutinized his patient, checking the NG tube, drips and listening to his labored breathing. "The impact caused trauma to his previous surgery and is also

165

affecting his inhalation and exhalation. It's almost impossible for him to find a comfortable place to rest."

"Give it to me straight. It can't be any worse than what I'm imagining." Would the impact of the accident undo everything he'd already been through? Six years ago, Kamilah had sat next to Reese's bedside following the mastectomy and hysterectomy. The mind-numbing pain he experienced then was overlaid with the hope this new body revealed the man underneath. The euphoria of the new birth fueled his healing.

"Mr. Thompkins is drugged up and in shock. He broke his sternum, two ribs, and has cracks in several vertebrae. He's broken the pinky finger on his right hand. There's a soft cast on his swollen right knee. The slightest movement is going to be painful. Can we sit at the table? It'll be easier to show you the x-rays of what we've found, the MRI, and the game plan."

Moving like a ninety-year-old Bermudian fisherwoman, she gingerly sat down in the chair giving her best access to the monitor. Kamilah was dealing with the aftermath of refusing to sleep in the adjoining bedroom last night. Her right hand automatically moved to the lower spine where her back was tight and screaming for its daily stretching exercises. She'd never spend another night in that chair.

"The MRI showed extensive damage and hairline fractures along his spine." The surgeon pulled up several screens until he found what he wanted.

He pointed out the minute cracks in the spine. Hairline fractures resembled tiny hairs. "Because he's going to be confined to the bed for a long time, the bones will press on the nerves, resulting in pain, tingling, and numbness. Depending on the severity of his case, surgery may be needed to correct this problem at some time in the future."

"He's already undergone so many surgeries. What's the binder for around his chest? Kamilah nibbled on her bottom lip as her mind replayed every day of the months Reese spent in the Belgrade hospital.

WINTER'S LAMENT

"He has a hematoma the size of a man's fist due to the blunt trauma to the body causing blood vessels to burst." He demonstrated by balling up his fist and pressing it against his breastbone. "See the reddish blue swelling. A hematoma this large is dangerous since it places pressure on the blood vessels and obstructs blood flow."

She nodded, unsure what to think or feel.

"He's having breathing difficulties. We'll have a surgical nurse in the room twenty-four-seven to manage it until we're convinced he can breathe without difficulty or if immediate surgery is indicated. It can take six to eight weeks for the hematoma to heal."

The tiny nurse seated next to Reese looked too fragile to do more than call for help. But if White Oaks said she could keep Reese immobilized, then so be it.

"Let me say this right now. Reese is going to have a long, slow, pain-filled recovery. He's going to require health care assistance after he's able to leave here."

"Are these new injuries going to work against the previous operations?" Kamilah, the caregiver, became the intercessor in the fight for her brother's life.

"There's extensive scar tissue from the hysterectomy. We're going to have to clean that up." The general surgeon acknowledged her concern.

A groggy Reese opened his eyes for a minute, grimaced and closed them again. The nurse was at his side, checking his vitals and wetting his mouth with a pink mouth syringe.

"How's your pain level from zero to ten with ten being the top," asked the surgeon? The surgeon's eyes automatically went to the machine tracking his vital signs.

"Fifteen." Tears flooded Reese's eyes, and strain lines bracketed the corners of his mouth. "Every inch of my body is screaming."

167

The surgeon walked over and stood at his patient's left side. He placed a hand on Reese's shoulder. Reese flinched and the doctor removed his hand. "Yours is a rare case, Thompkins. We don't have the expertise among our group to handle this by ourselves. We've located the best top surgeon in the country. He'll be here early this evening. He was consulting at a clinic outside Denver when we got the call from Dr. Overton."

Reese croaked, "Thanks."

"We're flying him in to consult with our oncologists. Your case is most like a breast cancer survivor with extensive scar tissue," the surgeon explained. "The blood flow from the hematoma must go somewhere. This man will help us figure out how to treat yours and any other problems we discover with less trial and error."

"The visiting surgeon asked us to perform a specialized mammogram because the area is cloudy. We've been in communication throughout the night, and we've sent him the films." The general surgeon leaned across the table and placed a hand over Kamilah's shaking hands. "The specialist will be up to speed by the time the limo from O'Hare drops him off here."

"He's experiencing too much pain everywhere." Kamilah stared at the moisture forming over Reese's top lip and him biting his lower lip. He'd do that for hours rather than ask for relief. Stoicism had its limits.

"He's thrown up on everyone," the nurse informed the doctor.

"Reese can't tolerate opium. When we were in Belgrade, they had to give him other drugs. What can you do to give him some relief until the top surgeon gets here?" Kamilah explained to the doctor and nurse what they'd discovered during his previous surgeries.

"We'll try some different cocktails. The best thing is to elevate his head and keep the air passages as clear as possible."

The general surgeon smiled his thanks, then spoke to the nurse. "We can't let him lie flat. It's too hard on his lungs. Both pain and the bed are his enemies. We also gotta start him on PT/OT as soon as we can regulate his pain. He's gonna have to work through it."

The nurse nodded and got up. She pulled a pillow out of the linen cabinet and gently placed it under his head.

Reese's face contorted with pain.

"We're gonna find out what he's made of," The surgeon said to the room at large.

"What do you remember, Reese?"

Five days after the accident, Reese was conscious, pain-wracked, and traumatized. He'd been prodded and poked. Asked stupid questions. The team members talked about him like he was a hospital dummy they were discussing to learn new medical techniques.

The general surgeon and his assembled team conducted a complete neurological exam, testing recall, mental status, cranial nerves, motor and sensory function, pupillary response, reflexes, and vital signs. The hematoma was not responding to repeated attempts to divert the blood flow. Once it shrank, his breathing would improve, and additional treatment could begin.

Reese needed assistance to stand up, to go to the bathroom, and to bathe. Once up, he walked a few steps with a cane and physical therapy staff assisting him. In addition to round-the-clock check-ins from clinic staff, the private duty nurse sat with him to ensure he was never alone.

Zende returned to Boston to begin preparation for one of his protegee's upcoming performance with the Boston

Conservatory at Berklee. He called daily to check on both Reese and Kamilah.

Kamilah was ordered to sleep in the bedroom attached to Reese's room since she refused to leave his side during the day. Meals were served in the rooms, and anything Kamilah needed was provided by the hospitality staff hired to deal with families of recovering patients.

Reese's pain was excruciating, yet he pieced together the accident for the neurosurgeon and orthopedist who kept peppering him with questions. He remembered the gas guzzler, the black ice, the impact of the crash and the second collision into the back of his truck.

He closed his eyes and let the scenes roll like a movie replaying on an endless loop. "Two good Samaritans called 911. I was drifting in and out of consciousness ...but I remember two men arguing about pulling me out. They were afraid the truck might catch on fire." He stopped, sucked in a painful breath, and stared at the specialists. He'd been poked and prodded, endured MRI and EKG and all manner of invasive tests.

"Shouldn't that information be in the report?" He'd tried to keep up with the doctors' back and forth debates about him before his records arrived from Belgrade. The Chicago-based doctors who'd treated him since the initial top surgery, came out to examine him and share his vital records. He was surprised they hadn't called in Dr. Erickson so the cast would be complete. His hands gripped the bed covers.

The specialists' laughter cut through the anxiety of the moment.

They have no idea what transpired in the hours before I got on the highway. In hindsight, I should have gotten a room at the W and slept for twenty-four hours to rid myself of the grimy final confrontation with Noori. Or maybe I should have been paying attention and saw that old guy cross the line in front of me.

The general surgeon who'd coordinated this group placed a hand on Reese's shoulder. "We're trying to determine what you remember, not what the report says, Mr. Thompkins." The medical team expressed concern about his bouts with anxiety and depression. "Thompkins, you need to keep still. It's a miracle you're not permanently incapacitated."

Reese licked his dry lips, and his voice cracked. One of the attendants moistened Reese's dry lips with the sponge. "...the Land Rover was still in Drive. I was wedged between the steering wheel and the airbags... I was fading in and out of consciousness." The attendant spooned ice chips into his mouth.

Reese smiled his thanks at the attendant and resumed his narration. "The doors didn't unlock because the engine was still on... I didn't feel my legs. The guys couldn't see my legs because the driver's side of the car was pushed in. My hands couldn't undo the seatbelts."

His eyes searched until they landed on Kamilah. "My clearest recall was Mommy appeared and sat on the cracked windshield. She kept telling me... *Baby, get out of the car. It's goin to be okay.*'"

Kamilah stared open-mouthed at him. The siblings often talked about his visions and his conversations with spirits.

"I know you don't believe me... but it was Mommy." Reese's faith allowed him to communicate with his parents. "Then a man's voice said, 'turn your head to the right. I'm gonna smash these windows and get you out.' The glass shattered... and the door flew up like an angel's wing."

Kamilah wept. She didn't have the same gifts but never discounted his.

"What happened to the two guys who hit me?" Reese's throbbing head and inability to move an inch without breaking out in a cold sweat kept him inwardly focused. He hadn't thought beyond his immediate pain, continuing negative information from the team of physicians, and uncertain recovery time.

"The guy who rammed into the back of you hit his head on impact. He was treated at the hospital and sent home with some powerful drugs. The driver who hit you head-on walked away without a scratch. He was drunk."

CHAPTER THIRTY-ONE:
NOORI

THE AMERICAN PSYCHIATRIC Association's unopened special delivery letter remained on Noori's desk until the staff, writers, and Voncile left after another problematic twelve-hour day. They were on a deadline for the promos advertising her new show. She'd been called out of a meeting with the staging crew because she had to sign for the letter personally. Her stomach clenched every time she glanced at the certified letter. Although clearing her name was a relief, the timing was lousy. Noori couldn't afford for anyone to connect *Time For Truth,* her groundbreaking show with this baseless complaint.

Noori was astounded by the APA's rapid response. She and her attorney expected the case to drag on and to eventually die from the lack of specificity. Without any physical evidence or corroborating witnesses, this was nothing but a she said/she said situation. Apparently, the combined clout of the university and Luna Erickson accounted for APA pushing through and responding to this pathetic grievance.

Noori slid the thin steel blade along the seam of the envelope and pulled out the single sheet of paper. She studied the contents, reading it three times, her eyes narrowing and her brain grinding to a halt. The language was crisp and professional. Guilty. Guilty. Guilty. She stared slack jaw at the contents of the letter. Guilty on all accounts. *Annorah Sherman, Ph.D., caused physical, emotional, and psychological harm to Reese Thompkins.* Yada. Yada. Yada. Her license was suspended for one hundred twenty days pending further examination of the case. She had the right to appeal the decision of the committee. If the suspension were justified, her psychologist's license would be permanently revoked. Without a license, she would be relegated to the sidelines of the sexuality debate. Credentials were paramount, and a diploma from an internationally accredited psychology program had been her ticket to the big time. That was in serious jeopardy.

With lead fingers, Noori replaced the letter in the envelope, opened her desk and pulled out a lock box. She punched in the code, and the top popped open. She slid the document in and closed the latch. *Hell. NO!* The temporarily defeated diva screamed and screamed until her throat was raw as images flowed through her brain of the committee members giving her the side-eye on numerous occasions during the hearings. How could a bad bitch like Noori Sherman have walked into the trap Erickson set and baited for her? Thompkins couldn't have pulled this coup off by himself. Erickson was jealous of Noori's success in mounting a campaign to reverse the result of research by Erickson and other liberals, particularly granting rights such as marriage to homosexuals.

Those damning transcripts. Her outbursts during the hearing were unforced errors, jeopardizing her position. Her lawyer had warned her, and she wouldn't heed his advice. Numerous committee members and bystanders in the hall saw her approach Thompkins for that private chat outside the meeting room. Thompkins knowingly provoked that scene because he was taping her without her permission.

The letter outlined the APA appeal process. Otherwise, the APA Psychologist's License Revocation would become final and the sanctions related to psychological harm to Reese Thompkins would be reported to the disciplinary database. And Luna Erickson would be the first person to publicly call Annorah Sherman, Ph.D. out in one of the scathing articles Erickson wrote for prominent research journals who so far had rejected Noori's research.

Noori hadn't had contact with her lawyer following the hearing, and she wasn't overeager to hear him say *"Do it my way this time around."* He was probably receiving this notice at the same time. She had four months to justify her actions. She didn't care which one of those shims he had to impeach to retract her confession.

Stop freaking out, Anorrah. A lot can happen in four months…one hundred twenty days. After this unmasking, ratings, interviews, and money would roll in. Her future would be set. Licensure would no longer be relevant. After the overwhelming disgrace of Reese Thompkins, she'd be clothed in dignity, asked to speak at numerous conferences, to consult, and to assist other churches in rooting out hidden sin. Her cheek twitched as her hands formed a steeple. With the money she'd earn, she would finally be free of Thaddeus Sherman. No longer stuck in Chicago, she'd be able to travel and live as she desired. *To all of you low-lifes who believed you had the last word on my behavior, I'm the victor.*

An hour later, Noori was still pacing the office and playing out victorious scenarios in her head. She needed a drink. But, with her father, Voncile and the production team hovering around, she'd taken to drinking fizzy water. The cameras picked up the slightest imperfections. Seething as she punched in the number, Thompkins picked up on the fourth ring.

"You were warned to stay away from me." The disembodied voice was strained and wheezy. She raised an eyebrow. No hello. No polite greeting.

She took a deep calming breath. "Getting my license suspended. You think you've won some major victory, don't you? I don't need any authorization. I have irrefutable evidence."

"Your last words to me were precise." Slowly, he repeated the words verbatim ending with, "what do you want, Noori?"

Although he couldn't see her, she stamped her feet. "Do. Not. Consider this is over. A lot can happen over the next one hundred twenty days."

"Noori, what will it take to make you crawl back into your hole and leave me alone." His voice sounded scratchy and distant as if he weren't listening to her. Thompkins seemed to drag the words out. "Not something I want to discuss over the telephone."

"Watch your back, Thompkins. I'm coming for you."

He disconnected the line.

***

Reese was dozing when the call came through. His intuition told him to let the phone go to voicemail. Kamilah had read him the contents of the letter earlier today. Then Dr. Erickson called, urging caution. "The APA will not render a final decision until Noori files her appeal." He'd informed her of his accident and long recovery time, swearing her to secrecy.

Zende had flown in to check on Milah as he did whenever he could schedule two days or a weekend away from his students. His contempt for Noori sometimes bordered on fury. He stood up and put his hands in his pockets. Noori's M.O. was predictable. Lash out. "You betta believe she's planning her next move in case the committee rules against her."

"Noori won't take this seriously. She'll try to twist it around to her advantage," Kamilah predicted. She placed the folder on the table.

"Guilty." While Reese was buoyed by the verdict, he had been through too many sleepless nights to celebrate this victory or to dismiss Noori's threats. "I don't give a damn what she does." His body was clammy with sweat. How she'd laugh if she saw him now. Reese needed a drink of water. He reached for the glass and sipped the cold liquid. "It's time to stand up and act like a man. She doesn't want a public discussion of her antics back then, or her continued bullying. As the face of The International Truth Institute, her behavior leaves them open to charges from others who may feel they're being targeted by these exposés."

Kamilah caressed Reese's fingers, taking care not to aggravate his injuries, silently reminding him of the plans to take his leave. "You can wait... finish your tasks here."

Until Zende hired Diamond, Reese hadn't fully appreciated the monster behind the façade. "I've had too many restless nights and too many tortured memories to let another person control my direction. It's finished. Part of being a man means standing up to bullies." Reese had to lighten his load if he was going to heal. "Zende, get in contact with Noori." He eyed Zende pacing back and forth like a caged lion. "Regardless of what the APA does, I'll meet with her in any forum she chooses."

"We'll make the arrangements." Zende stroked his chin and nodded his assent.

Kamilah and Zende shared a look. "Are you healthy enough physically to do this?"

"God's timing is now!"

CHAPTER THIRTY-TWO:
REESE

REESE'S RIBS WERE HEALING. His eyes were no longer bruised, and the hematoma was finally responding to treatment. He'd lost weight and resembled a young Michael Jackson without the curly hair or the sparkly white glove. He shuffled down the corridor of the psychology wing with the aid of a new prototype walker which allowed him to stand upright rather than hunched over like a shuffling senior citizen. After repeating the MRI, the doctors determined there was not enough change in the hairline fractures. Therefore, the binding was still in place.

Daily physical and occupational therapy intensified the throbbing throughout his body. Instead of the agony, he focused on the colorful outdoor scenes and the pastoral setting. No one would imagine this oasis was thirty minutes away from downtown Chicago. He was drawn to his destination by the musical sounds of the German composer, Bach, and swore Doc Bailey used the captivating music like the Pied Piper when persuading children to run away from their ordinary lives.

By the time he entered the therapist's comfortable office with its matching couch and chairs in oatmeal leather, every nerve ending screamed like Aretha singing "STOP" in the Blues Brothers movie. He lowered himself into a chair especially designed to minimize his discomfort and wriggled around trying to discover a comfortable position. He rubbed his knees and sucked it up.

Doc Bailey, a gray-haired, sixtyish woman with large eyeglasses, sat in the orange office chair behind the kidney-shaped desk with an all-in-one computer and printer. Its well-worn leather conformed to her body. Today she was wearing a purple sweater over a loose, black scooped-neck dress which showed off her red, blotchy chest and low-heeled pumps. She sounded nothing like Dr. Erickson with her Midwestern flat vowels and downstate Illinois Air Force brat take-no-prisoners attitude.

"Come into my garden." Doc chuckled. Her tone was upbeat today. A good sign for him. An armoire that doubled as a stand for the television and bookcases overflowed with roses, honeysuckle, and passion flowers. They were diverse and beautiful at the same time. They overpowered the usual smell of lavender Reese associated with Doc's office. "It's my wedding anniversary, and since it's a workday, we're saving the celebration for the weekend."

"Happy anniversary, Doc." Reese swore she blushed. He lowered himself into a straight-back chair. Easier to get out of at the end of the session when his muscles tightened up again.

"My husband got carried away." Doc looked him up and down and nodded. Then she addressed Reese as always: stern, no-nonsense, and straightforward. "When we first started these sessions, you were hesitant. We've finally gotten comfortable enough to discuss the results of your tests. You have Post Traumatic Stress Disorder... PTSD. A very severe case of PTSD."

Reese exhaled and remembered the adage, *a physician who treats himself has a fool for a patient.* During his Master of Divinity program, he'd taken pastoral care classes and knew the technical definition and signs of PTSD. He'd encouraged Grace and the staff to make concerted efforts to work with marginalized kids in the congregation and with adults who were suffering from various traumas. But, to his reasoning, he was atypical. He could handle the stress, the confusion, and the terrors. He'd spent years micromanaging his actions to avoid returning to his earliest traumas when kids taunted him, parents refused to let their kids play with him, and he lived in fear of assault, rape, and death. He assumed he'd dealt with it all during therapy, only to slide back into the very thoughts, conversations, places, people, and activities which triggered old memories.

Doc's next words snapped him back to the present. "Tell me how you fought and achieved a major victory by undergoing surgery to complete a physical transformation and then stopped going to therapy. You know better than most how difficult the inward transition is. You needed time to assimilate to your new body. I even understand why you postponed the bottom surgery, but not for five years."

Reese's skeletal system ached. He shifted around, rubbing his knees. Because the only way to heal was to let the poison out, Reese opened his mouth and uttered the words he'd dammed up for five years. "While in Belgrade, I continued individual and group therapy after the surgery. Some of the other guys were disowned by their families, harassed, and threatened as word of their transition spread. I stopped participating, trusting I could manage on my own. After several months, I started waking up with night sweats and night terrors. I swam miles each morning, composed music, and totally disconnected from the truth during the daytime."

Doc coughed to clear her throat and said the words he'd heard before. "That's regressing, not moving forward. Living openly as a man before the transition enabled you to build the skills for living in your new body. Yet, you created a sham marriage, injured your sister and made a mockery of everything you hold sacred." The therapist leaned into him and touched his clammy hands. "Anything you did to avoid dealing with the real problem was just another form of self-medicating and distancing yourself from the real issue." There was no judgment in her voice. Only understanding.

Reese pulled his hand back and replied through the emotional pain. "Inward transitioning takes a toll, like on the Illinois Freeway. There's no end to the toll payments. And the cost keeps going up. Folks saw this hot male body. Often, I overheard them saying *I want some of that hot chocolate.* That is not what I was experiencing...the masquerade was easier. I couldn't do it alone. The fear immobilized me. I was dodging landmines at church and in my personal life and running out of excuses to Kamilah about why I couldn't let her go."

Doc spread her hands out to him. "Reese, you can't hide from yourself, and you can't hide from God. What I don't understand is why you involved Kamilah. She's been a hostage to your drama. You manipulated her. Did you ever consider how unraveling this sham marriage would ruin her life in the process?"

Reese held his fist in front of his mouth, studying her. He bit his fist and spoke through his clenched teeth. "Selfishness and self-centeredness define my life. And arrogance. It's hard to say it to myself, let alone to you. I cared more about my needs than I did about my sister's. Although it crippled Milah's spirit, secretly, I was glad Zende didn't come back." He dropped his gaze, studying the pattern of her office rug. "I needed Kamilah's strength, her presence and with him out of the way, we were inseparable again. When Milah decided to attend college in Savannah, I was forced to make friends and grow up. But always in the back of my mind, I knew she was nearby whenever I needed her."

Doc frowned at his comment. Her eyes shot daggers at him. "Kamilah's always been your shield and protector, but she's a real person. She has needs and desires for her own life, including a career, marriage, and children. Friends even." She pointed a stubby finger at him. "You've got to let her go. Immediately."

Reese felt attacked and tried to deflect his anger. "Zende deserted her, and now he wants to whisk her away like none of that happened."

Doc jabbed back at him, the Air Force brashness punctuating every syllable. "Reese, you're not that selfish. Kamilah loves Zende. If Zende's not good enough for her, how can she meet a decent man while you keep her tied to you?" Doc stared at him until he dropped his eyes and his foolish pride. "There are sickos out there who'd distort your relationship as incestuous? Even Noori Sherman is endeavoring to smear you and spread malicious lies about Kamilah. You've put her in an indefensible position."

A weary Reese couldn't refute any of her statements and harsh words. He'd rebuked his self-serving behavior repeatedly. Now it was time for action "We debated how to end the charade for over a year. Milah applied and was accepted into the Ph.D. program at Sofia University in California. I was headed back to Serbia. I'd written my letter of resignation, and then the tornado hit."

"The tornado became a convenient rationalization. There were others who could've taken cues from you as you made your transition." Doc was relentless in her assessment of his underlying motivation.

"My ego got in the way. How could I walk away when the people needed me?" At the end of the day, Reese's plan failed miserably. Now he needed time to reprocess and integrate new information, stop lying to himself and get over the fear.

"Now that's delusional. There's always going to be a need or a new catastrophe." Doc closed her eyes and massaged the tension at the bridge of her nose. "My favorite cliché is the road to hell is paved with good intentions."

Reese inhaled the scent of the flowers and let Bach's "Mass In B Minor" settle into his soul. "I believe if the deacons had listened to me, we would have rebuilt the Tower and I'd be gone."

Doc blew out a string of expletives. "All that good and necessary activity still hinders you from dealing with you. And that's what you and I are going to do." Doc glanced at her watch and back at him. "Lasting trauma affects how we deal with new situations, good or bad. Some people believe one round of therapy will cure PTSD. With each forward movement, you're taking a new risk. You got to let go."

"Yes, ma'am," Reese agreed. He gazed out the window, letting the serenity of the place work its magic on him. Peace and tranquility. Even with the changing seasons, tornadoes, storms, snow, drought, the trees continued to thrive. Some were pruned. Some died. But they endured.

"Twenty plus years of fear, navigating real and imaginary threats took a toll on you. Just like vaccinations, Reese, you needed booster shots which you overlooked. You needed therapy before the walls rose to box out the light. Surgery was one step. Living a new reality was the second step. Start by telling me why an attractive, ambitious, talented man who's into women is too scared to live the life he fought so hard to gain?"

Reese's mouth worked, trying to form the words around the pain in his chest. It felt like his inner walls were crumbling. He was scared and fearful of shutting down again. He gripped the arms of the chair. "I'm stuck. I was battered and almost raped by a group of thugs when I was a young teen. Zende and his friends saved me. There were older guys in the theatre who tried to pressure me into having sex in exchange for the hormone treatments I needed. I had to be shrewd to avoid them. By the time I came stateside, I had perfected the image and constructed the barriers."

"This sham life is an escape. You're like the tortoise. You stick your head out and don't like what you see. Then you tuck your head back in your shell. Your instinct is to reach for Kamilah and avoid the apparent signs of distress that manifests itself in irritable bowel syndrome and the other disorders you suffer from."

Reese nodded.

"It's time to live a new reality without shackling Kamilah. Let your sister live where she's not numb and isolated. There's no reason for either of you to be in a rural community. It's inconsistent with everything you've experienced or know to be realistic for a man with your gifts and resources."

"How?"

"You always think you have to do more. That's guilt. Stop it. You've done so much for the church and its members that you're afraid to do for yourself." Doc Bailey said, "You paid a heavy price for the deception in ruining your physical health and isolation. You opened yourself up to blackmail and coercion." She rattled the facts off, her eyes sympathetic but unrelenting. "Your assignment is to openly talk about who you are and the transition process. Tell your church. Don't let this woman distort the truth. If you want to help others, stand in your reality. Get it over with quickly so you can heal."

Reese nodded.

"Then, I want you to go out and meet women. There's no reason for people to know you're transgendered. However, when you meet someone, catch feelings, but before you become seriously involved with a woman, tell her the truth. Let her decide if she can handle it. Your partner needs to respect you, your body and your choices."

"I'm not sure how to do that." He shook his head sadly.

"You don't know how because you haven't had any intimate partners since the transition. You haven't allowed yourself to feel desire, to love anyone. I'm not minimizing attacks and rejection, but you went overboard on secrecy and personal safety. I need you to stop reading negative stories and start living."

"Okay." The old discomfort reared its head.

"There's no going back. Think about what you're going to do, how you are going to step up and be a man."

Doc should have been a mind reader. Nothing got past her.

"You're too young to be living a life of regrets. You made decisions with the information you had at the time. Now you're trying to reinterpret those decisions based on the man you are today."

Reese grabbed for the lifeline she offered him. She stood, signaling the end of their time together. "Our work together until you leave here is about how to disentangle you from this situation with the least amount of damage to Kamilah. I'm also going to spend some time with her."

CHAPTER THIRTY-THREE:
KAMILAH

ALTHOUGH REESE HAD PHYSICAL therapy daily, he wasn't strong enough to walk the grounds without assistance yet. The siblings sat in the solarium, his only link to the outside world. Today Kamilah updated him on the financial campaign report she'd received earlier during FaceTime with the high-spirited fundraising team. Each time the red thermometer in the lobby inched closer to five million dollars, the congregation celebrated, thanked God and additional members made financial gifts. Deacon Slay and Rev. Thornton were keeping a lock on Deacon Grimm now that his employment status was public knowledge. His personal issues were consuming more of his time than church business. Grimm was savvy enough to maintain his credibility with the congregation and backed down, although he'd contributed nothing to the project. Hudson and White grudgingly made donations after being convicted by their friends.

Outside the thunder boomed and Reese winced. He moved, easing the ache in his chest, and letting his lungs fill to full capacity. "How near are we to closing out the campaign?"

"We're at 4.2 million dollars. Deacon Slay wants to close out the campaign." She read from the notes she'd scribbled during the meeting. "The hitch is none of the team sees a way to make it across the finish line without you in a visible leadership role." She'd exhausted her personal contacts and auctioned off a few paintings to raise money for the project

Reese mused for a couple of minutes, then chuckled. "This is what Doc Bailey keeps drilling in my skull. *There'll*

186

always be another crisis, another situation." He swiped at his moist eyes. "The last twenty percent is always the hardest to acquire." He put his head in his hands and pondered for a long moment. When he glanced up, she knew he had a plan. "I've still got royalty money from the last two albums. Use the money to set up a two to one match. For every two dollars, the committee can raise, I'll match it until we reach the targeted five million dollars."

Kamilah leaned back and gave him the side-eye. "You're willing to spend over $250,000 of your own money to make this happen."

Reese shrugged nonchalantly. "I own one hundred acres of land surrounding the music studio. Regardless of where I end up, $250,000 is an investment in keeping my work alive and vibrant."

"I don't understand." She wanted desperately to have this mess all behind them. It seemed as if there was a new roadblock with every step Reese took to free himself of this melodrama.

He handed her a marked-up contract document. "Doc Bailey and I've been drafting a concrete plan for me to disconnect from The Cathedral which includes investors taking over the studio and the production company."

She scanned the contract. "You're really going to let the studio go?" She stared at the paper as if expecting to see another way out.

"Yes, I am." His smile reached his eyes. She laid her head on his shoulder. He touched her face gently. "It's gonna be all right. Now go and talk to Doc."

***

Rain poured down. The day was a misty gray, gloomy, with no sun, and a heavy mist. Even so, Kamilah would have preferred to be outside than sitting across from Doc Bailey. "My leg aches when the weather's like this." She stretched her leg, rubbing it. "Days like today, I miss Bermuda. Mommy used to say the hot sun bakes away whatever's ailing a body."

Doc's finely tuned senses kept Kamilah from sliding out of facing facts. In here she was able to speak about her deepest feelings. "You miss your mother, don't you?"

Milah bowed her head. "Dealing with life's challenges never stops. I need Mommy to tell me how to fix this mess Reese and I made of our lives. When Chaz Bono made his public transition, Cher was by his side the whole time. She couldn't shield him from public humiliation and shame because of her celebrity status. Yet her being there was comforting and a blessing for him." Milah leaned back in her seat and closed her eyes, placing her folded arms across her chest.

Doc slid her chair closer. The two women shared long conversations where Milah was able to connect the pieces of memory she'd discarded along the way. Doc Bailey left her chair and sat next to Kamilah on the small sofa. Doc handed her a wad of tissues and waited until Kamilah composed herself. "Milah, when your parents left on the cruise ship, they intended to be home in a couple of weeks. You've fulfilled your promise. It's time to let Reese go. He's stronger than he was at fourteen. He'll always need you, but he needs to witness about what he's living through. He won't fall. And if he does, he'll call out, and you'll be there to pick him up." She patted Milah's hands.

Kamilah's mouth firmed into a line as she stared at Doc. Tears streamed down her face. Her hands clenching and unclenching, nodding, hearing the words again. A teen's promise to her parents. Finally listening and understanding when Doc said *It's time for you to step away.*

"Your parents didn't intend for you to sacrifice your life for Reese's. They didn't know those words would be their last message to you. It's time to deal with your own issues. You've never dealt with your life-altering accident or your boyfriend who needed to grow up. He's returned and wants to make a covenant with you."

"I don't know how." While she'd dated several men while living in Savannah, her mind was clear. The men were temporary. And she couldn't stand it now if Zende's obligations to his family overruled his love for her.

"You're ready to let go of your emotional and physical reactions to Reese's transition, your internalization of a message in a way your mother never intended and sacrificing your life for Reese. Choose you. Choose Zende and in doing so, let Reese go. He'll stumble, but he'll survive. He always does. He's working on a plan. One he won't share except in tiny bites because I made him put his big boy pants on."

After her morning exercise workout and walk around the tranquil gardens, Kamilah either sat with her nose in a book or sketching new pictures with adult versions of the three children from her earlier works. The answer to which *boy* she'd chosen was evident in the touching of hands, interlocked arms, or the tender embraces the two adults shared. When all three were together, the scenes were peaceful and the smiles affirming. Kamilah paused after the final sketch realizing Zende was the love of her life. She was ready to step out on shared faith in their love. With his acceptance of the siblings' unique bond, Zende became less of a threat and more of an ally. Kamilah powered through the daily messages from The Cathedral, only involving Reese when necessary. On a subliminal level, the cord was being cut. Deacon Slay and Rev. Thornton were managing the day-to-day operations with input from the senior staff.

Grace was providing updates on Genesis. Her father, Frank, finally stepped up and hired a high-profile lawyer for her. On the day before the case went to trial, both sides agreed to a settlement. Calvin pleaded guilty to a misdemeanor of criminal sexual assault, the equivalent of statutory rape. He'd serve up to one year in jail where he could take correspondence classes. The convicted rapist then had one year of probation while continuing to take college classes. He had to file as a sexual offender. If he didn't commit any other offenses, he might lose the sexual offender designation. Genesis lost weight and was not eating well. Just as she had been unthinking and mean to other kids, they were now whispering about her. Even her BFF Tayshaun had given a negative statement about her to Calvin's lawyer without mentioning Pastor Reese's name. The teen was required to participate in a court-ordered mental health treatment program with a specialist who counseled her and Misty. Misty was learning behavioral expectations must be specific as well as the consequences for bad behavior. You can't punish a kid into good behavior. The only bright spot in Genesis' life was her court-ordered volunteer hours spent at the hospital's neo-natal unit. She was learning the extreme possibilities of what it meant to have and care for an infant rather than the made-for-television movies she loved to watch.

CHAPTER THIRTY-FOUR: REESE

REESE TOLD KAMILAH AND Zende, "It's time to move on." As a result of continually coughing to keep fluids from building up in his chest, Reese's voice remained hoarse. He tried to maneuver his emaciated body out of the hospital bed. Zende and Kamilah grabbed each of his arms, restraining him, pushing him back onto the narrow bed. Reese watched the lovers growing closer. Zende flew in from Boston every weekend to give Milah support. Time had healed the old wounds, and they were planning their future together.

Reese knew gossip swirling around The Cathedral had him badly disfigured or in drug rehab. No car accident required this much time away from the church or the Gospel Choir. There was a lot of grumbling and complaining because the members weren't sure about the extent of his injuries. They weren't allowed to visit him. Although there had been regular updates about his progress since the accident, some members raised questions about Reese's continued absence from the pulpit.

Kamilah and the Head Deacon talked daily. If Reese wasn't in therapy, he listened in. "Don't worry about The Cathedral. Rev. Thornton stepped up. He, Deacon Slay, and Grace are keeping Grimm and Hudson in check. Deacon Slay told Marcelle Grimm to shut up before he told the congregation he lost his job due to excessive gambling."

Reese's chest hurt too much to laugh. "Not true."

Kamilah kissed his cheek and wiped away the moisture from his eyes. "Slay is a master game player. Marcelle did lose his job, and he is a gambler. He figured you hadn't told Rev. Thornton about the deacons' threats."

Reese marveled at the older man's tenacity, his ability to defuse Marcelle Grimm's treachery to hide his shortcomings. "How is Deacon Slay?"

"Still going to dialysis and praying for a kidney. Steadily moving up on the donor list."

Kamilah reminded him. "The general surgeon says you need more physical therapy before you're ready to leave here because he knows you won't put in as much effort on your own. You'll fall back into old habits. No clinic or surgery in our area is equipped to provide the comprehensive care you need."

"In addition to these new injuries," Reese spoke with an edge to his voice, "there's the hole in my gut I've been attempting to fill with antacids from agonizing over what my congregation thinks of me or what society will do to ridicule and minimize my ministry."

"Ulcers can be fixed," Zende told him.

"I'd invested too much time and energy in agonizing over how Noori could twist my situation for her own purposes." Reese's mind raced ahead to contemplate a brighter future. "Doc and I sorted out some of my issues." Reese lifted his head. "Through God's grace, a true healer discovered my secret and refused to profit from it."

Kamilah cocked her head as she watched him straighten up in the bed. Rather than hover, she was learning to let him do things his way and on his own time. "I've added Dr. Overton to my daily prayer list. There were multiple ways to manipulate the situation. He could've let the hospital gossips have a mega-fest at your expense. He could have sold your story to the tabloids or worse."

Although he raised his eyebrows at her faith in the goodness of men, Zende smiled at his woman. "Overton was concerned about his hospital's reputation. While they might have gained a little notoriety in the short run, the backlash would've been severe. LGBTQ advocacy groups are vigilant about these kinds of civil rights violations. It's costly for hospitals to implement required training for all its personnel."

He shot Zende a scowl. "Not a perfect world. I'm grateful to have this sanctuary. In the middle of the night, God whispered to me as He has so many times before, *'there's a balm in Gilead to heal the sin-sick soul.'*" Reese changed positions, easing the pain in his chest, and settled on the bed. "My injuries will take more months to heal. There's no way I coulda risked being in adversarial surroundings."

"Yo, right, man."

"Once I handle my business at The Cathedral, I'm returning here for more physical therapy. Then I'm headed back to the clinic in Belgrade to finish what I started." Reese pointed to a folder on the tray next to the bed. "Zende, pass the folder to Kamilah."

Zende did as he was told, looking over her shoulder as she read the papers. She looked up at her brother with questions on her lips and in her eyes.

Reese shushed her before she could start. "My lawyer and financial advisor will deal with The Cathedral around a disposition of my contract, real property, and the production studio."

Kamilah looked at Reese out of the side of her eye. "When did you do this?" The report was thorough detailing information from the inception of The Gospel Choir, a listing of all property, real and intellectual, and financial accounting by a CPA.

"Sometimes in the middle of the night. I hear you snoring." He mimicked her loud snores. "The studio's owned jointly by you and me. I've had offers over the years to sell or take on a partner, but I was enjoying making music too much. I suggest you sell it. If you want to wait a while, Jimmy's a capable manager and can hold the group together. We're not going to see my work stolen by some unscrupulous clowns because they think the scandal weakens me. Some of the talent and the producers will jump ship. Hold them to the noncompete and nondisclosure agreements, and intellectual property clauses."

Zende craned his neck toward Reese. "You know it's not over." Kamilah and Zende were keeping their ears to the ground. The private investigator had someone tailing Noori while they waited for her to show her hand. The P.I. was also analyzing Noori's increasingly disjointed blogs.

Reese cleared his throat as he stared back at Zende. "I want you two to represent me at the Stellar Awards. Whether I win or lose, do what needs to be done to promote our brand. I'll pick up the pieces later." Setting his affairs in order was the best thing to come out of the soul-searching. He made some excellent business decisions and was able to leave Kamilah with everything she needed financially. It was the least he could do for her years of sacrifice.

Kamilah realized Doc Bailey had spoken the truth. Reese had a definite plan, and he wasn't going to slide back into denial. She waggled her fingers in his direction, smiling as she thumbed through the actions he'd taken.

CHAPTER THIRTY-FIVE:
REESE

NOORI REFUSED HIS OFFER of a settlement conference. Reese had been out of the pulpit for two months when Diamond's operatives learned about Noori's television contract and the secretiveness of her debut show. Based on who her other targets were, Diamond figured the production company was planning an ambush as soon as Reese was back in the pulpit.

Following the plan Reese and Doc Bailey laid out, he'd written out his resignation letter and let Deacon Slay know he would be in the pulpit on Sunday morning to deliver it. Diamond also uncovered an insider at The Cathedral tipped off Noori that Reese was returning. Reese refused to allow the people he'd relied on for the past five years and who he loved like family to hear his story at the same time as the congregation. Last night, he'd assembled his inner circle. The people Reese trusted most: Deacon Slay, Dr. Thornton, Grace, and several other members of his cabinet, arrived at the Winston House on Saturday evening to spend the night in a prayer vigil with him, Kamilah, and Zende. They prayed and sang before he painstakingly told the story of his journey and his next steps.

Rielle Thompkins was born the second daughter to Luke and Saraya Thompkins, traveling actors, musicians, and backup singers from Defuniak Springs, Florida. Like millions of other entertainers who never rose to the top of the industry, they moved from place to place seeking work. They signed a one-year contract with a cabaret in Bermuda. Six months in, they decided to stay in Bermuda permanently and become members of the island troupe catering to tourists year-round. Their girls needed permanency and an education.

Talented kids, Rielle, and Kamilah lived among the other artists in the group, observing performers create illusions day after day. Rielle especially loved creating music, playing any instrument left untended for a minute, and mimicking every song her parents sang. Kamilah's talents were in writing stories and illustrating them, often capturing the actors in less than favorable poses, and dancing. Given the hectic life of the theater, the two youngsters learned how to make-up the artists, dress the performers, and keep track of wigs. If someone didn't show, they might be called on to substitute in a bit part.

The theater, the imaginary lives of actors, the larger than life performers were just what Rielle needed. Many of the talented thespians they lived and worked around were also mentally ill, alcoholics, drug addicted, homosexual, and trans. Yet everyone had a burning desire to create experiences that transcended the humdrum of daily life, to lift people up, make them laugh, and to occasionally make them think beyond their ordinary boring lives.

Shortly after her fourth birthday, the precocious little girl cut off her long curls, dressed in jeans and a plaid shirt, and blurted out to her dumbfounded, incoherent parents, "I'm a boy. My name is Reese." Luke and Saraya's was a family stitched together with love. As entertainers, they witnessed unusual couplings and pairings, dissolutions of marriages, gay, lesbian, and straight relationships. They knew Little Reese fit somewhere on that continuum. From that moment on, Rielle disappeared. Reese dressed and acted like a boy because that's who he was inside. He developed a swagger and had his hair cut in a bald fade. His thick unibrow was trimmed, and he appeared more masculine.

Around the theater, Reese befriended all the men in the theater family such that he knew who was taking hormones to grow boobs and how they hid their junk. In exchange for him helping with odd jobs and cleaning rooms, "Who do you think cleans and orders that shitty pigsty where we live?" and cooking food, they taught Reese how to bind his budding breasts and walk as if he was packing. "Don't do that uncivilized shit ... touching your stuff." From them and underground sources, Reese obtained testosterone hormones he needed to deepen his voice and purchased the "packer", a device simulating a male bulge. Reese's uninhibited chatter with transvestites, trans men and women was the equivalent of group counseling with licensed therapists without the moralizing and second-guessing. Reese's big, soulful eyes would beg for information. The guys answered questions and didn't judge.

Rev. Winston designed The Winston House's large living room for entertaining distinguished guests. The room with pale blue/gray walls was huge with luxuriously carpeted floors, coordinated sofas, and chairs set up as conversational groupings scattered around the room, expensive art on the walls. The cafeteria staff had prepared a sumptuous meal and set it up in the dining room. The intimate group, some seated in chairs, some on the floor eating and drinking gallons of coffee or other drinks. They asked questions, talked strategy, and made plans for The Cathedral's future. The energy levels rose and waned as the inky darkness gave way to the brilliant reds and oranges of sunrise. No one had slept more than a couple of hours. Finally, the group moved to their bedrooms to shower, dress, and sit at the dining room table where they nibbled on breakfast foods before corporate prayer and making their way to the house of God. Although there would be loose ends to tie up, God's house would not be torn to pieces by one preacher's actions or the vengeance of a demented woman.

Reese's energy was zapped by the time he slid into his Cole Haan loafers. By the time he entered The Cathedral, he sat quietly behind his office desk until the disembodied security chief's voice rumbled in Reese's earbud. "Cruella de Ville is on the move. She's traveling with a national film crew and her biggest backers. She'll be on the property in approximately sixty minutes. It's Show Time."

Reese's clipped voice recapped the plan. He gave orders to the security team. "Lock the front gates. Post a guard to tell them no visitors allowed today. Send all the young people to the Winston House with Grace and the youth ministry staff. We're starting service in ten minutes. Once the congregation's seated, lock the doors. Do not admit stragglers." Although walking without the cane was strenuous, Reese's swag returned.

"Are you sure you're up to this?" Kamilah looked him up and down, hugged him, and kissed his cheek. "Remember, the doctor says you're not physically cleared to return to work."

Deacon Slay's smile was still cemented on his features, and he whispered in Reese's ear. "My wife and I pray for you day and night. We hope you'll take what you pour into these people and let it guide you."

Reese crossed his arms and lifted an eyebrow at the beloved elder.

Slay reminded him. "*Get Out of the Boat* was one of yo best messages."

"Reese mumbled the words, "No fear. No assuming what comes next. Focus on Jesus. Believe His word. You won't be free until you step out on faith, believing with your heart ..." Reese hugged the elder. He pulled back and looked at his expressive face and smiled weakly.

Reese communicated with security via his earpiece. "Can someone set Zende and Kamilah down front in her usual place?" This morning's drama-filled event was his best plan to be rid of Noori once and for all. "Zende," he extended a hand to his rediscovered friend, "keep your hands off my *wife* for a few more minutes." His muffled laugh was sorrowful. Back in the moment, he continued speaking to security. "Text all nurses, medics, little play nurses, doctors, and healthcare providers in the house. Tell them to spread themselves around the congregation. We're going to need them today. It will become self-evident once the service begins."

Reese punched in his Communications Director's code. "Tanji, it's going to be Improv at The Cathedral in the sanctuary this morning. I don't have a clue about what visitors are going to show up or how their visit is going to end. Let's follow our script but remain flexible."

"We got you, Pastor."

"Noori's group is on the highway now. We're not giving her a heads-up. Turn on the cameras. Shut off all the external feeds. We'll roll the entire service later today, with Noori included once I've calmed down enough to record an intro segment."

"I'm gonna miss you." Tanji's voice was full of admiration.

"I'm gonna miss you, too." Reese surrounded himself with a team of people who had fallen in ditches and got back up. They were less judgmental than the folks who never deviated from the straight and narrow lives prescribed for them. "Key up the special video. Today is the day we settle this once and for all." Reese sucked in air to calm himself down. "The musicians know to follow my lead exclusively when I walk in. Be ready to go with the flow. We have one shot to do this right."

For the last time, Reese fell on his knees in his office, closed his eyes, and clasped his hands through the throbbing agony. "*Lord, your people need a word from You this morning. You told me to come as you are. I came as a broken person, in sin and shame. You met me at my point of need and washed me white as snow. I'm the vessel. The words are Yours. When I walk in there, it will be my testimony, my truth. Hold me. Love me. Lift me up. And when it's all over, I'll be careful to give You all the praise.*"

Ten minutes later, Reese entered the sanctuary, wearing a new European cut black suit and crisp white shirt to conceal the weight loss and black tie. Gold cufflinks blinked at his wrists as he stood in the opened sanctuary door. The congregation had never seen Pastor Reese on a Sunday morning without his trademark robe. Without the cane, he hobbled down the sanctuary's center aisle. He climbed the stairs cautiously, holding on to the stair railing until he reached the stage and walked to the podium. The ministerial staff flanked Reese, some with wet eyes, others holding their Bibles aloft in a symbol of prayer and steadfastness. He pulled out a handkerchief and wiped his moist face.

"Good morning, saints." Pastor Reese's voice was resonant although he'd spent all the previous night talking and praying, plus the added misery of hiking down the aisle and up the stairs to stand before them. "This morning, I'm going to share my testimony." He stretched out both hands toward the unsettled congregation who sensed something amiss. The whispers and murmurs ratcheted up a notch. "Undoubtedly, some of you will leave this ministry as soon as you hear my testimony. Follow your heart about how you deal with the information I'm sharing." He looked out at the sea of stunned faces, whispers, and heads shaking negatively. Reese paid attention to the hunched shoulders and heard the murmurings. Folks were leaning in closer. His preaching voice rose above the congregation and gained their attention. "I was called to serve The Cathedral's people. When you can no longer perform the job, it's time to go. There's no need for a prolonged fight to rip apart the fabric of the ministry." He gestured to the staff surrounding him. "My resignation letter is on Deacon Slay's desk. These able anointed leaders will carry on in God's name." Reese reached for the glass of water and sipped. He winked at Kamilah's radiant face. She gave him a small thumbs up. Tuning into the messages flying over his earpiece, he had fifteen minutes before the shit hit the fan. He continued. "I was born a man ...but I was born in the body of a woman."

Reese stared into the sad eyes of Deacon Slay who'd prayed with him all last night. Today was testing Deacon Slay's faith notions he had about manhood and God's anointed. The older man endeavored to practice the belief that God's love doesn't have loopholes. Gasps came from some of the deacons. Slay raised his hand for quiet and stared into hostile faces.

"At age four, I told my sainted mother 'Something's not right. God forgot to give me a penis.' She sought professional help. The doctors advised her to learn as much as she could about what it meant to be transgender. They counseled her to allow me to lead the conversation and the actions. Being a spiritual woman, she followed her heart."

Kamilah and Zende smiled encouragingly to counteract the open hostility and rage bombarding Reese from others around the sanctuary. "Living on an island, little kids wore cut-offs and t-shirts, so clothing wasn't the issue. When I kept butchering my hair, Mommy finally took me to the barbershop and got me a buzz cut. Enough of the backstory." The impact of his announcement shook the foundation of The Cathedral. Some folks sat back in their comfortable chairs treating his life story like a concert or lecture, depending on their personal beliefs. Others reached for their phones. The noise level increased ten-fold. His preaching voice rang out across the stunned crowd. "Please hold your texts and tweets until I finish. Then you're free to do your thing." He stood still for a minute as fingers stilled over the devices. Calm and order descended on the members of the congregation. "Before you run and tell, make sure you have all the facts first. You don't want to have to apologize for spreading half-truths on Facebook and Twitter when you can tell the whole story first time out the gate."

A few people high-fived each other. Some looked ashamed, knowing they'd planned to be the first to leak the news coming out The Cathedral. *"Girl you should be in church right now."*

"Y'all better Christians on Facebook than you are in real life." Reese's teasing words lessened the tension, fear, and pain reverberating around the room. "Kamilah is my sister. She's three years older than me." Mouths opened and closed. Fish lips were on display, especially among a group of women who had tried to tempt him with their womanly wiles over the years. "Part of why I'm telling you in this way, without preparing you is because I need to set Kamilah free." His throat fisted. "She has to be liberated to live the life she gave up for me. More importantly, she needs to be free to build a life with the other man who's also loved her all his life." He extended his hand to Milah. "Can you forgive me?"

Kamilah was openly weeping. Members of the congregation stared at Kamilah and Zende as recognition dawned in their eyes. Zende put his arm around her, pulled out a snowy white handkerchief and dabbed at her eyes. "Our parents not only loved me, they understood me and my great need to have my body, identity, and mind aligned. Poppi and Mommy sacrificed, knowing we couldn't leave Bermuda and return to Defuniak Springs, Florida because of prejudice and the fear of harm caused by people who didn't understand or accept my differences. "Milah's been a ferocious protector. Y'all think Beyoncé's Sasha Fierce is something out of this world. She can't hold a candle to Kamilah."

Her beaming, teary face provided the reassurance he needed. He acknowledged Zende with a salute and a thumbs up. "My biggest critic and foe Zende Lightbourn arrived during the winter storm. He got me thinking about how to untangle this mess I'd created. How can I lead when I'm constantly looking over my shoulder waiting for the other person who knows my story to humiliate me and destroy this place in the process?"

Inquisitive eyes and open mouths hung on to his words. There was more to the story than being a trans man.

WINTER'S LAMENT

"Recently the woman came here on a sneak mission to figure out how much damage she could cause. Her mission failed, but she found an ally in the church family. Someone who's been feeding her information about my recent absence." Boos bounced off the walls around the sanctuary. "Dr. Sherman's traveling here now with a television crew and people who want to humiliate me publically. In the process, they intend to ruin this church. The Cathedral is a beacon for all God's children." He raised his hands up to quiet the noise. "God will judge me, and I will accept His judgment."

"Amen, Brother Pastor." Some members weren't willing to let God pass judgment. Tight lips, frowns, and ugly faces stared back at him. Groups of people were holding hands as tears rained down their faces.

Reese checked his watch as he listened to the warning from the security coming through his earpiece. "While she's getting ready to storm in here with her national cameras, we don't have time for questions and answers. However, if you're willing to stick around a little while after the show, I'll answer your questions. "For you to understand who this woman is, I've prepared a short video. It provides a snippet of my journey, my relationship with this woman, the surgery, and its aftermath. When the video ends, security will open the door, and the next voice you hear will be Dr. Annorah Sherman, spokesperson for the International Truth Institute, whose mission is to destroy clergy who don't live up to their standards. Roll the video."

CHAPTER THIRTY-SIX:
NOORI

"*It's Time for Truth.*" Three of Noori's bodyguards rushed the sanctuary door as soon as The Cathedral's security guards stepped away to allow them entrance. With a camera-ready smile, Dr. Annorah Sherman strutted into the room. For her national debut, Noori was immaculately groomed in a purple suit with a cream-colored silk blouse and black five-inch Jimmy Choo's. Her Tamron Hall hairstyle complemented her features, and a traveling make-up artist had professionally applied cosmetics flattering her skin tone and clothing. Her strong forward momentum froze. Noori stared up at the three oversized screens showing the same picture of her: in bed, naked, her happy face up close and personal with Reese's before the transition. Noori screeched, "Shut down the cameras!"

Dr. Thaddeus Sherman, marching in lockstep to her left, gasped, "Blasphemy. The devil is a liar." A deep shade of crimson spread up from his neck to his face and bald head.

Mrs. Portia Sherman's eyes rolled back in her head as she slumped to the floor. Medical personnel rushed to Mrs. Sherman to administer smelling salts as she moaned and groaned on the carpeted floor.

The six-man film crew dressed in black with microphones on poles, rolling lights, and hand-held cameras continued documenting the chaotic scene. Cameras snapped around the sanctuary as The Cathedral's members either snickered, laughed, booed, or pointed fingers at Noori and back at the frozen screen. Noori's backers and entourage's jaws dropped as they witnessed the screenshot.

Reese signaled for the screens to go black. The Cathedral's security team coerced the frenzied entourage back into the lobby and slammed the sanctuary doors.

When Portia Sherman was able to stand with the assistance of an on-site physician, The Cathedral's security guards directed Noori and her mother into Reese's private office. The security guard addressed Noori. "Pastor said for you to wait here. He's got something to say to you." They were shown to the bathroom to compose themselves.

Harrison Lord's florid face contorted, saliva dribbling from the corners of his mouth. Sherman's business partner and influential backer punched his fingers into Sherman's chest. "What the hell happened in there, Sherman? You told us the bastard was going up in flames."

Sherman's wild eyes skittered around the room. He pushed the man away, shrieking, "A traitor from our end must have tipped him off. Someone spliced the film to create those offensive images."

The head of the camera crew, Harold Gunn, skinny with a greasy ponytail, was irate. "Somebody better come up with an explanation for the network. I don't think Judas and the thirty pieces of silver gonna work this time."

Sherman grumbled, "I'll murder whoever defamed my daughter."

The crew chief, sparing a brief glance at Sherman, didn't try to hide his laughter. "Your backers were expecting a different kind of expose. There's a press conference scheduled at 3:00 p.m. today."

"A lot of wasted money and effort." Lord squirmed and cleared his throat.

Sherman's crowning achievement was ending in dismal failure. "Damn prick pulled the rug out from under us."

CHAPTER THIRTY-SEVEN:
REESE

PACING BACK AND FORTH behind the podium, Reese's flashing eyes inspected the sanctuary, which was now three-quarters full. While security expelled the intruders, certain members scurried out as soon as the doors opened to eject the trespassers. The musicians soothed the crowd with Richard Smallwood's *"Praise Is What I Do."* The uproar at the back of the sanctuary died down. Social media was alive with audio and video and varying accounts of what was happening at The Cathedral. Reese raised his arms for quiet. "I promised to answer your questions." His pain-wracked body was operating on adrenalin. He mouthed *"pain pills"* to Kamilah. A moment later, an usher brought his pain meds to him. He took the pills, chasing them with water. He watched as questioning members stood up and pointed to the three microphones placed strategically around the sanctuary. "Use the microphones in each aisle. This is not a dialogue session. State your question and then take your seat."

Moving swiftly, old, and young, formed long lines at each of the three stationary microphones. Over the next forty-five minutes, Reese was physically and psychically exhausted as he answered numerous questions. His chest hurt. His knee throbbed. He'd squelched a panic attack or two under the sharp scrutiny of some of his members. When he could no longer ignore the severe pain in his chest, Reese shut off the microphones. He moved to the podium for one last word. Some considerate soul poured fresh orange juice and placed two more pain pills next to it. His eyes sought out Kamilah. He nodded in gratitude. "There's a group of people outside the walls of this church who need me. Folks who've been taught God doesn't love them because of their gender identity or sexual orientation. Children and adolescents who are the victims of discrimination, violence, abuse, and degradation daily. Teens and young adults are selling their bodies for drugs, for a place to sleep, or for a moment of connection and human kindness." Clapping and cheering erupted from one section of the house. Another part sat stone-faced.

"God reminded me that I was selfish and ungrateful. *Sceered* as the kids say." Eyeing each other, the young adults pumped their fists. "It's way past time to stand in my truth." Reese staggered from behind the podium and slowly plodded the perimeter of the raised platform. It was the only way to deal with the excruciating pain in his body. The clergy associates stood with him. Each one touched his arm as he passed by, filling him with strength and comfort. "Whether you accept me or not, I've got to shine a spotlight on the greatness of God."

"Ouch, pastor," someone yelled from the upper balcony.

"Thanks, Sam." Sam's struggle was one of living openly regardless of what people called him. He wore skirts or pants as the mood suited him. Sam wore his long hair in a feminine style. He carried a purse. Sam refused to accept labels of queer, gay, or crossdresser, instead saying, "My name is Sam." The outcry lessened the tension in Reese's soul. "When I go walking down your street, say *ouch*." A little laughter and he recovered his edge, his purpose. Reese's words reminded the fractured congregation, "We've all fallen short. All sinned. Some of you are saying to yourselves, and to those around you, Pastor's sin is gigantic... greater than anything I ever did."

A few brave souls nodded. He dropped to one knee, unable to support the injured joint any longer. "I've failed you. God says a sin is a sin. There's no hierarchy."

"Double ouch."

"My sin was not in being transgendered." Reese stopped. Rev. Thornton hugged him and helped him up. "My sin was living in fear. For being arrogant. For not having faith in your capacity to accept a transgendered man who loved God."

"We love you, Pastor."

"Don't go."

"Please stay."

"Ouch."

"If I hadn't been so terrified of the naysayers, I might've helped someone else who's going through the same journey without the remarkable family support I had." Reese dropped his head. When he lifted it, his eyes were glassy. He couldn't distinguish faces. "Family support didn't make other kids accept me or save me from adult bullying." Reese needed Kamilah's strength to get him over the finish line. "My biggest transgression was clinging to the person who loved me unconditionally. I lived beneath God's promise." Tears leaked out of his eyes and rolled down his face. He did not attempt to stop them. Come up here, Milah." He extended both hands to her. Kamilah stood, regal in her black and white geometrically striped dress. Accompanied by Zende, she walked up the steps to join Reese on the podium. Kamilah's formidable presence gave him the will to finish. "God's favor is not fair. He's given me more than my share of unmerited support in the form of the person who understood a little kid's rantings when she discovered she didn't have a penis, about God making a mistake, and could we please ask Him to fix it. She never left me, never tried to change me. Over the years she offered advice I didn't take, yet she loved me, supported me and this ministry. Her contributions are too numerous to mention."

Kamilah's arms enfolded him. She hugged and kissed him. Their tears mingled. "Milah, your acceptance of me was the best validation of my identity. You taught me about compassion." She stood next to him, holding his hand, lending him potency for the final words. "I'm leaving you with a solid, dedicated ministerial staff who can manage under Rev.

Thornton's leadership. He, his wife, and kids have been with us since the beginning. Give him a chance to see what he can do."

Members wept throughout the sanctuary.

"Your money is straight. The auditors will be here in the morning to begin a special audit the deacons commissioned so some of the naysayers," he stared down at Deacon Grimm, "cannot say I vanished with your money or exited leaving you in debt."

"Ouch."

"Finally, I leave you with the five million dollars in the bank you raised for rebuilding the Tower. The money's in a designated account and can only be used for the project. I signed the papers ... and paid the non-refundable deposits to the contractors."

Cheers! Hoots! Laughter!

"Go with God just as I will. When the Tower rises again, remember God's love is paramount. Pastors come and go, but God is steadfast. I hope to see you in the rapture." Reese and Kamilah with Zende following behind them walked down the steps and up the center aisle leaving behind a stunned congregation.

CHAPTER THIRTY-EIGHT: REESE

SOCIAL MEDIA WAS LIT up with the drama playing out at The Cathedral as Reese limped into his office, followed by Kamilah and Zende. Pictures from this morning's service of Pastor Reese, Zende and Kamilah, Noori and Thaddeus Sherman flashed across the screens strategically placed around the office. The commentary was mixed. Pro and con for Pastor Reese, Dr. Annorah Sherman, and The International Truth Institute. A disheveled Portia Sherman, shock marring her beautiful features and professional make-up ruined by tear stains, sat slumped in Kamilah's favorite chair. Tanji had given her an icepack and a steaming cup of herbal tea. Thaddeus Sherman's f-bombs lit up the air. The hypocritical façade had been stripped bare. His reputation was forever tarnished when social media revealed he was the mastermind behind the controversial International Truth Institute. Sherman had conspired with his daughter to destroy The Cathedral and its pastor.

Noori paced the room, alternately screeching and crying as allegations against her swirled on social media. Noori's female lovers came forward with tangible evidence of multiple same-sex relationships. When Reese entered the room, she rushed toward him, the stench of alcohol enveloping her. Her hands fisted to beat on his chest. "You tricked me."

Reese grabbed both her hands and pushed her away from him as if flinging away a pesky puppy. He leaned against the wall, winded. "Let's say, you were never holding all the cards.

You were too busy trying to screw me over to remember significant portions of our time together or your real life."

"Huh, what are you talking about?" Noori's neck veins stood out. She was at stroke levels if her labored breathing and perspiration-soaked clothing were any indication. Her eyes were unfocused. Her speech slurred. "Nobody will hire you when I get through smearing you in the media. I'm gonna own that production studio you love so much."

Reese pointed the water bottle in her general direction. "Over the past couple of months, I've had nothing but time to think straight, to put bits and pieces of conversations together. I called and spoke to the other two guys you tried to entrap."

"Two more losers," Noori huffed.

Kamilah reached out to grab her, but Tanji and Zende held her arms. "Reese has this under control."

"Annorah, stop this. Right now!" Her mother's low-pitched voice barked, clutching her pearls as copious tears rolled down her face, ruining her designer suit.

"Give it a rest, Mother. This piece of roadkill is beneath the shit the housekeeper scrapes off the toilet," Noori said with a bite. "Who cares what happens to him?"

"You called me 'him.'" Reese's cryptic laugh made others in the room turn to look at them. "Progress."

Thaddeus' slumped shoulders bore the weight of years of closing his eyes to what was in front of him, of listening to and believing his daughter's lies and evasions.

Reese took Noori's hand and kissed her knuckles. Noori wrenched her hand away. "You're soulless. You use vulnerable people. It's not about your father, or research or," he mocked her, "the homosexual agenda."

Portia's mouth was hanging open. She was following every word spoken between her daughter and this preacher.

"You were ambiguous about your own sexuality. What better place to *experiment* than with people whose lives are

212

chaotic or in disarray. Where you could control everything." Reese winked at her as she ground her teeth.

Thaddeus listened to their exchange; his face was darker than storm clouds. He blasted Noori, "We warned you if there were any negative consequences, they would be on your head."

"This is not my fault," Noori whined like a little girl wanting her daddy's favor instead of the fanged she-wolf she usually presented herself as.

Reese looked at the older man's outraged face, beetled brows, and snarling lips. "Your daughter is not a truth teller." His voice held no sympathy for the man who'd thrown him out of his home and precipitated the events leading up to this overdue showdown. "You shouldn't be surprised. You pay her to twist the truth for a living."

Sherman's flush started at his neck and moved to the top of his dome-like head.

Reese stated, "Although this wasn't her intent, Noori taught me I could connect with another human being. So, as the Book says: you meant it for evil, but God meant it for good."

Noori bellowed, "Stop quoting scripture to me."

Reese's head was clear, and the wound was excised. "I wanted you to stick around so I could deliver the message personally. I'm not waiting for the university or the APA to issue a final ruling on the case. I'm taking my life back and to hell with what you choose to do after today."

"You'll be the laughingstock of the planet."

Reese shrugged, "Somebody's going to ask why it took nine months of sex with another 'female' for you to figure out you were in the same kind of sexual relationship you rail about in your blogs. Do you have an answer for them?" Reese turned to Thaddeus. "While you were investigating preachers' lifestyles and sins, you should've paid more attention to your daughter's sexuality. It's amazing what you can learn by talking to her friends. Go back and ask some of her high school buddies what happened on those ski trips and other vacations. I'm sure your Institute could do some research and share it with the world."

Sherman's jaw clenched. He raised his fists. Kamilah stepped between Reese and Thaddeus Sherman. "Y'all need to leave. My brother's recovering from a serious car accident."

Thaddeus' head whipped toward Noori. "There was nothing in the media about an accident."

"Why do you care? Would you have been kinder, softer, or less offensive in wrecking my life?" Reese asked. The challenge went unanswered. "The world knows I'm a trans man. You've done what you set out to do."

CHAPTER THIRTY-NINE: REESE

WHEN REESE BOARDED THE plane for Serbia, he was on his own for the second time in his life. Determined to do it right this time around. He was ecstatic for Kamilah and Zende, who'd flown to Vegas for a quick wedding ceremony he could share with them. Their lives had changed in remarkable ways. He loved how Zende was spoiling her. Then, they headed to Bermuda where Zende's mother was planning another elaborate ceremony and reception for them before they returned to Palo Alto and Sofia University.

Reese gazed at the water's edge. The clinic sat high on a cliff above where the Danube and Sava Rivers connected. The peaceful spot with land rising on either side had become his place for communing with God. Reese and Kamilah had Face Timed at least once a week during the nine months he'd been in Serbia. It was his way of keeping her updated on his progress. "Milah, I'm checking out of the clinic tomorrow. The penile implant surgery's complete. No complications."

"It's finally over." Milah's infectious laughter and sparkling eyes flashed across the screen. "We're so proud of how far you've come, physically and emotionally."

When he lifted his head, Kamilah's cheeky grin filled the screen. She'd encouraged him to make friends, to be open and honest with any woman he might be interested in forming a relationship with. "Tremendous. Acknowledging my scars instead of hiding them with an elaborate masquerade. I pushed through the terror and refused to let Noori destroy me."

Kamilah shot him a thumbs up.

Working with a therapist, Reese sorted out some of the reasons he'd made the mistake of living a lie. "I didn't realize how closed off I was, how scared I was. I created a protective barrier that was wrenched away. Now it's just me in my naked glory. I exorcized the enemy inside my head through music and words. The book deal ... and the music deal both point out the deceptive behaviors many people have and the pain they mask. The book lays it all bare. Nothing hidden. Mistakes and all. The connecting thread is letting God lead me and telling everyone God is there for you, whatever your need. My story also expresses undying gratitude to Mommy, Poppi, and to you."

"Don't make me cry." Kamilah sniffed.

Reese ran his hand over the jacket of the book his editor had sent him with the last set of edits. He turned the jacket cover, and it filled the screen.

"OOOOOOh." She squealed.

"The final proofs have been returned to the publisher. My agent is lining up the talk show and college circuit for me. Based on pre-sales and advance marketing, the book will release at the top of the New York Times and USA Today Best Sellers' Lists. I'll do book signings and talk to people about what this journey is about."

"We're so happy for you."

"God's message to me has always been that His love doesn't discriminate. He created me, loved me, and held me up through all my doubts and fears. My new truthful life is learning to be a single man and walking in my purpose." One day Reese would find the one woman for him. Until then he was okay.

"Call me to come and vet all the honeys." Milah's teasing voice was like a warm benediction around him.

"Absolutely."

"When are you coming home? LA's our primary location until I finish the degree. We have more than enough room for you at either place."

"Soon. I'm heading to New York for prepping for the tour. I'll be finding a place to lease for a while. Most of the Gospel Choir's gonna join me on tour. I've been texting and chatting with them. They love the new music and the chance to be on another international tour."

Kamilah's radiant face was close to the FaceTime screen. Reese could feel her energy pulsing around her. She asked, "Did your lawyers resolve the suit against the Truth Institute? What's happening with Noori?"

Reese received the final papers last week. Another reason he could move on. "Noori lost her professional license. Significant sponsors pulled out once the modified show aired. Her own team turned against her and provided footage from inside The Cathedral. The mess on Facebook and Twitter didn't help. She's gone underground for now. She'll surface again. That kind of hatred doesn't go away without some life-altering change." Reese continued. "Her professional liability insurance company and The International Truth Institute paid hefty fines to me and smaller amounts to the other two men. The Institute filed for bankruptcy reorganization. Sherman's finances were tied to the Institute. He's scrambling to stay afloat." Walking away hadn't ended Reese's linkages with The Cathedral. "My lawyer and financial advisors are dealing with The Cathedral around a disposition of the real property and the production studio." He owned a portion of the land. He was still making money for them, and they didn't want to lose the income. He'd tried to be fair, but they were going to have to let it go. Reese was not allowing disputes over money get in the way of his new life. Reese's voice dropped an octave. "I need one favor."

"Anything for you."

"Let's begin the book tour and first concert in Los Angeles. You and Zende can host it. All his friends must purchase copies. We'll donate the proceeds to the charity of your choice."

"Yes. All the glory belongs to God."

Made in the USA
Columbia, SC
03 July 2020

13085052R00136